"Katlyn's first [obscured by barcode] path to redemp[obscured] Ethan Grey. Her words bring to life a love story worth reading from cover to cover. You will find yourself laughing and crying along with the characters in this book."

- Tiffany Campbell, Texas Mother of Two

"Katlyn Grace writes with a very gentle but poignant spirit. In *Finding Hope*, Ethan Grey is a very broken person, and Katlyn managed to keep his character a wonderful and caring hero, despite his struggles. I can't wait to read the upcoming books in *The Lawson Series*!"

- Cleopatra Margot, Author of the *Faith to Love Series*

"*Finding Hope* is beautifully written. Katlyn Grace writes with elegance and spirit. Ethan is a lost soul who needs help. Hope is a baker with a spiritual purpose in mind for him. God has a plan for them both."

- Tawnya Hanna, Homeschool Mother of Two

"*Finding Hope* kept me on the edge of my seat from the very first sentence to the last.

This novel is truly an inspiring love story centered around faith, strength, and hope. Can't wait for more!"

- Adison Woods, Wesleyan College Student

"I couldn't turn the pages in *Finding Hope* fast enough. This story was packed full of faith, flavor, and fun. Katlyn Grace did a marvelous job at proving there is hope for anyone. I can't wait for the rest of *The Lawson Series* to come out!"

- Charity Faith, Abeka Homeschool Student and Owner of @CharityFaithBakes Instagram

Finding

Hope

KATLYN GRACE

Finding Hope

Copyright © 2019 by Katlyn Grace

ISBN: 9781699804537

Unless otherwise indicated, Scripture quotations are from:

King James Version Bible

© 1611

dedication

THIS BOOK IS DEDICATED TO MY PARENTS. I WOULD NOT BE HERE IF IT WAS NOT FOR THEIR CONTINUOUS LOVE AND SUPPORT. ALL MY LOVE GOES OUT TO THEIR SPECIAL HEARTS. THANK YOU FOR EVERYTHING, MOM AND DAD.

FINDING HOPE

"...hope we have as an anchor of the soul..."

Hebrews 6:19

FINDING HOPE

prologue

He downed one last shot of whisky and straightened his spine. His sister's words still rang in his ears. *You are what people would call hopeless, Ethan. You're hopeless.*

It stung. He was letting her down and he knew it. Ethan was letting himself down, but he was too far in now. His sister had been right…there was no hope for him. Even if he tried, he'd never be the person he used to be—before the alcohol. Before all the pain.

He tipped the bartender ever so generously and stumbled out into the brisk, chilly night. The dark resembled his insides. He felt alone tonight. Alone and depressed. It had been exactly three years since his parents died in that horrific car accident. It also had been three years since Ethan was sober enough to carry along a conversation and awake enough to even know what was going on around him.

How had his life gotten this low? It was miserable. He was doing everything he knew was wrong, yet never strained himself to fix it.

But no. There was no point in trying to fix something that shattered into a million pieces three years ago. He already lost his family. His sister practically disowned him after last night. What did he have to live for?

Nothing, he believed, *absolutely nothing*.

one

"**M**ark's message was absolutely beautiful yesterday." Hope flashed back to the sermon her older brother had preached for Sunday morning church service.

She rolled another piece of fondant out and cut it into squares. *Waiting on God.* It was a subject so dear to her, and her brother seemed to touch the very heart of it. *Song of Solomon 2:7, "I charge you, O ye daughters of Jerusalem, by the roes, and by the hinds of the field, that ye stir not up, nor awake my love, till he please."* She'd been repeating the scripture in her head constantly ever since her brother preached on it.

None of Hope's past relationships had been a smooth sail, to say the least. She always thought it was the timing that had been bad, but maybe it was the fact that she hadn't ever waited on God. She always felt the need to rush and take the chance if an opportunity was presented. She never gave God room for what *He* thought was best.

After Mark's sermon, Hope decided to alter her narrow point of view. There was no room for her to straddle the fence between what she thought and what God thought. God's plans would surely give her the best results. So, she decided to wait on Him. There was no better relief than to solely place her future in the hands of an all-knowing God.

"It was. Mark has grown so much in the ministry over the past couple of months. God has something special planned for him," Hope's younger sister and best friend, Brianna, replied with a beam spread across her face.

"Considering he's not running over anyone's toes with his battery-operated Mustang anymore, I'd say he has matured." Hope giggled at the childhood memory. As a kid, Mark never failed to show off for the ladies in his sleek little black Mustang. Hope

4

just always happened to be in the way when her smooth big brother did so.

"Oh, memories." Brianna sighed with a laugh. "Do you want me to start boxing the sugar cookies for the Richmond's birthday party?" Bri asked her sister as she pointed to the blue Superman cookies.

"Pretty please with a cherry on top." Hope batted her long eyelashes as Brianna maneuvered her way through the kitchen toward the boxes.

"You're pathetic," Bri teased as Hope laughed at how she always managed to sweet talk her little sister into boxing all the goodies.

They went back to work in a peaceful silence, or at least as quiet as their bakery kitchen could get. Refrigerators hummed, and timers buzzed. Brianna boxed desserts and Hope decorated a gorgeous wedding cake. She added various shades of mint colored flowers to cascade down the right side of the white three-tiered cake.

Anne, who worked the counter at Hope and Bri's café and bakery, pushed open the swinging doors that separated the café from the kitchen. "Hope, he's out there again." She barely spoke above a hushed whisper.

Hope wasn't surprised. The town drunk was there just about every morning, always hungover.

She quickly wiped off her hands on a towel. "Anne, if you wouldn't care to help Bri finish boxing those cookies, I can handle the counter for now." She smiled and pulled off her polka dotted apron and pushed through the doors that lead to the café part of her bakery.

Funfetti Café and Bakery was surprisingly quiet for eight o'clock in the morning. They were normally swamped at this hour for scones, coffee, muffins—all the breakfast essentials.

She scanned the room. Two business looking men discussed something at a booth in the corner, and a father and his child shared a fresh cinnamon roll by the wide floor to ceiling windows. Glancing toward the bar stools near the display case, she spotted him. In the same seat he always sat in. Hunched over, with his left hand holding his head up. His soft, brown curls weren't long, but they still framed the sides of his face, and his green eyes were hazy.

6

Ethan Grey.

She swore if this man wasn't the alcoholic that he was, she would be interested in him. Hope wasn't going to deny the fact that with a little cleaning up—including shaving—Ethan wouldn't be that bad looking of a guy. To be frank, he didn't even look terrible now. Plus, he was wealthy too, but money didn't solve all problems. He needed to get in church and put God first, then maybe she'd consider it.

Hope mentally kicked herself for even thinking about such things. As gut-wrenching as it was, she knew this man was far from any of that. He was quite the opposite of what she looked for in a guy.

Ethan's heavy breathing alarmed Hope, but she tried to look past it. "What can I get you this morning, Ethan?" She brushed her bangs out of her face.

"The usual," he replied, taking off his leather jacket and setting it on the barstool next to him.

Hope nodded and headed to the display counter showcasing all Funfetti Café and Bakery's delicious goodies. She pulled out a double chocolate chip muffin, wrapped it in a fancy brown paper, and slid it across the counter to him. She then proceeded to pour out a fresh cup of black coffee, adding no cream or sugar. *Strong*. She knew this man like the back of her hand now…at least his orders anyway.

"Thanks." He nodded at her as he handed over cash, already knowing the amount before she could say anything. He ordered the same thing every morning.

Hope saw the desperation in Ethan's stormy eyes. It was as if they were screaming, "*Help me, I'm desperate*." Hope could physically see how miserable he looked. Something pulled at her heartstrings and she found herself wanting to talk to him, to discover the reason why, and help him with his addiction. She couldn't help it, that was the type of person she was. She wanted others to know that there *was* hope.

She kept herself occupied behind the counter by putting on fresh pots of coffee, refilling the donut section, and wiping down the white marble countertops.

"It's awful gloomy outside today." Ethan's voice surprised her. He was trying to make small talk with her.

She glanced out the windows, catching a glimpse of the dark, puffy clouds. It had been sunny when she had left her apartment. Now the rain was slashing down. "Yes, it is." She glanced back at Ethan. Fine lines defined a frown at the corners of his mouth. Tear stained cheeks had his face looking a bit red this morning. His dark and weary eyes met Hope's. He wanted to talk, and she wanted more than anything to see him smile.

She sighed and took a seat opposite of him on a barstool at her side of the counter. "So, you've been coming here for about two and a half years almost every morning." Hope paused to make sure she had his attention. "Are my muffins just that good or what?"

His lips curled into a small smile. A tiny dimple formed at the crook of his mouth that Hope had never noticed before. "Your bakery is a great way to start the day." He took a sip of his coffee. "Although, I think I am going to have to discover a new muffin flavor. After three years of double chocolate chip, it's not that special anymore."

Hope grinned. *Keep him talking,* she told herself.

"Are you sure you don't want to change up your coffee order either? We even have a butter pecan flavoring now," she teased him. Black coffee was just nasty. Hope at least needed a splash of milk and a dash of sugar to even consider drinking it.

He chuckled at her remark. "There's nothing like a good ole cup of strong joe."

Hope relaxed. Ethan wasn't as intimidating as she thought. She suddenly wanted to know more about him, like what made him an alcoholic, what his reasons were behind his actions. Those would be questions for another time, though. She didn't want to scare him off first thing.

"Tell you what, tomorrow morning when you come, I'll have a whole lineup of muffins for you to sample. You can pick out your next muffin to eat for the upcoming two and a half years," she offered with a smile. She knew generosity would be the only way to open this guy's heart, and she planned on doing just that.

His eyes that were once dull, sparkled for a moment. Hope was delighted to see a rare smile like that on his face. "Count me in," he replied, wrapping his fingers around his warm mug.

"Good. My sister and I will be here at six in the morning to start prepping. Be here thirty minutes after, and I'll let you in early." Hope hopped off the barstool at the sound of her sister calling her through the kitchen doors.

"Sounds like work is calling you." He seemed amused as he took another swig of coffee.

"It's never ending around here." Hope grabbed a muffin for herself from the display case. "Nice to chat with you, Ethan." She disappeared through the double doors and went back to work.

The rest of her day flew by and before Hope knew it, she was back in her apartment.

It was a snug apartment. The only rooms that were hidden behind walls were her bedroom and bathroom, creating an open floor plan that made her apartment seem bigger than it was. Hope tried for the most part to stay neat. Although, she was a sucker for new pillows. Where there was a place for one, she most certainly had a fun, decorative pillow. Her kitchen was the biggest and most

11

used area in her apartment by far. She accented her airy white colored rooms with plenty of pastel colors. Her apartment was…girly, *very* girly.

The clock on the microwave in her kitchen told her it was 6:00 P.M. Her brother, Mark, had promised to come over this evening and grill steaks for the two of them. It was nice having a big brother who protected and genuinely cared for her. He was a police chief, therefore protecting was his job, but being an older brother to two sisters took that job to another level. Bri and Hope were dear to him, and he always made sure to show that through his actions and words.

Hope smiled at the thought of him. She was incredibly blessed.

She set the cardboard box of leftover cupcakes from her bakery on the counter for the two of them to devour after dinner. There was no way they were eating dinner without dessert. She figured Mark's gigantic sweet tooth would appreciate that.

Hope placed garlic and parmesan crusted potatoes in the oven to bake, then headed to the shower to clean up. She wouldn't dare eat dinner with flour and fondant caked in her hair and on her clothes.

She picked at a clump of crusty buttercream icing on her shirt. She found that Mondays were the busiest cake making and decorating days, also the messiest. She giggled at the sight of herself in the mirror. She was an absolute mess. There was no way Mark was seeing her like this, for she'd never hear the end of his teasing.

Mark had come over an hour later after Hope had finished blow drying her hair. Dinner was delicious, but mostly eaten in silence, as they were both starved.

They were now settled on the couch to watch the Chicago Bears play the Pittsburg Steelers. It was the third quarter and the Steelers were beating the Bears to a pulp. The disgusted look on Mark's face said it all. Hope had to admit; it was awful to see their own team losing.

"I can't even bare to watch this." He turned the volume down on the television. "Want another cupcake?" He gestured toward the seven cupcakes left in the box as he took one, leaving only six.

Hope snarled her nose and shook her head, declining the offer. "I don't know where you're putting room for all of those cupcakes. Especially after eating steak, potatoes, and veggies." Hope had only eaten one and a half cupcakes, so that left Mark to have already eaten three, working on his fourth. She silently chuckled.

"Cupcakes are your specialty, especially these banana cream filled ones. You have stepped up your game, Sista." He took another bite of the cupcake. "I might have to stop by and grab a dozen for the guys back at work tomorrow morning. They'll go crazy over them."

"Free cupcakes, who wouldn't love them?" Hope laughed. "Speaking of tomorrow…Ethan Grey. Do you know him?" She bit her lip, wondering if she was crazy to even bother bringing the subject up.

Her brother quirked an eyebrow at Ethan's name. "I think everyone knows Alton, Illinois' town drunk." He grabbed another cupcake. "Why?"

"He normally comes to the shop every morning, hungover, but never says a word. Today, he started a conversation with me."

14

The color drained from her brother's face and he sat his cupcake back down. "What did he do?" Hope watched Mark switch into big brother protector mode.

"Nothing, I promise," she answered. Instant relief washed over Mark's face. "I could just see the desperation in his eyes, though. Everything about him screamed *help*, like there was a better person inside of him just begging to crawl out. So, I offered to let him sample some muffins tomorrow morning as an excuse to possibly get to know him better. A way to see a reason through his actions."

Mark nodded, knowing that this was the kind of person that Hope was. She saw hope where others didn't. He told her earlier that he was beginning to see the significance of her name with her personality. "I just want you to be careful and listen to whatever God tells you to do. In the book of Colossians, it says to put on kindness, humbleness of mind, and so on, but above all, charity. You never know, what you do or say might just lead him to God.

"People like Ethan aren't just alcoholics. There's more to his story, whether it be anger raging inside of him, sadness, or a family issue. Maybe he even feels alone and depressed." Mark turned to face her, his big brown eyes making direct contact with her green ones. "Hope, you're good at seeing the best in others, I've noticed that a lot recently. Take the talent that God's given you and put it to beneficial use."

She blushed at his compliment, "Thank you, Mark." She grabbed blankets for the two of them and wrapped herself in one.

"I think God's pretty pleased with you," she mentioned, grabbing Mark's attention.

"I'd like to think so, but why you mention it?" He shifted his attention from the football game to her.

"Bri and I had to drop off some cookies for Billy Richmond's birthday. He turned eight today. You know who he said he wanted to be like when he grew up?" She asked him with a grin.

There was a pause, and then Mark finally asked, "Who?"

"His entire birthday party was themed around Superman, yet he said he wanted to be just like you. *He wanted to preach for Jesus and see people saved.*" Hope repeated what Billy told her, word for word.

Her brother's eyes lit up and crinkles lined the edges of his smile. He shook his head in disbelief. "I don't know what to say."

"You're inspiring people that you barely even know. It's amazing." She poked his rib. Proud was an understatement. There wasn't even a word to describe her emotions toward her brother.

"It's nothing I've done. It's all God." He leaned back into the couch and refocused on the football game.

Any girl would be lucky to have Hope's brother as a husband. He not only stood on good family morals, was a cop, and pastor, but she'd be lying if she said he wasn't handsome. His chocolate colored eyes and cocoa hair had a charm that kept the ladies turning heads. He had women turning his direction ever since Hope was old enough to remember. Their mom had always said that Mark got the charm from his dad. She smiled and shook her head at the thought. Maybe some of his luck would rub off on her.

"I've got to go. My team is losing, and it's past my bedtime." Mark groaned, frustrated with the fact that the Bears were losing bad. The score was now forty-seven to fourteen. She grimaced. It was a bad night to be a Bears fan.

"Get out of my home. You're getting grumpy," she teased. "But take the rest of the cupcakes with you, I can't bear to eat another one." Hope held her stomach at the thought of even taking a small bite out of one.

"I have no problem with that." He snatched the cardboard bakery box and his coat. "Thanks, Lobster." He smirked at the nickname. He had given it to her at the age of ten because of her strawberry blonde hair, and occasionally called her by it when he wanted to aggravate her.

Hope swatted his side. "I hate that nickname and you know it."

Mark's mission to annoy her was accomplished. "And with that, I'll be leaving." He laughed opening the door.

"Goodnight, Squirt." She chuckled and closed the door behind him.

She loved her family.

two

He rolled over on his bed only to have the sun hit him directly in the face. Ethan winced. There came the headache. He was used to it by now. A couple of Tylenol would do the job. He stumbled with his footing as he rolled out of bed. He caught a glimpse of his answering machine by the bed and saw that it was blinking red from a new message.

Ethan pressed play. "Ethan, if you could give me a call, I'd greatly appreciate it." He didn't recognize the phone number, but the voice sounded like his one and only sister. For some reason, she sounded weak and desperate. He rolled his eyes. He was not in the mood to even think about Sara, let alone talk to her.

Their last conversation had not gone over well. He had already been drunk when she dialed his number. Sara had begged him to quit drinking and living life like it was some sort of game. She even offered to pay for therapy for him to recover and become the person he once used to be.

The thing was, she didn't understand. Alcohol was his only way of escaping the realities of life. It was his chance to forget the past, and completely lose himself.

Of course, Ethan refused and told her to stay out of his life. That's when she told him he was hopeless, and those words hurt him for some reason. It was like taking a knife and cutting him down the middle.

Ethan was supposed to be taking care of his sister. His parents would have wanted that. More than that, his parents have wanted him to keep God in his life. If they were here, he'd still be coaching the high school boys' soccer team. His life wouldn't be a mess, and he could possibly be happy.

Happiness. Joy. Peace. He had forgotten what it was like to be happy. It was hard to be happy though when your parents were snatched away from you at the age of twenty-two. That was the cause of Sara turning her back on God. Their mom was Sara's best friend, and for God to take that person out of her life, it made her angry.

It was easier now for Ethan to tell himself that if God were real, He would have stopped the eighteen-wheeler with shot brakes from barging into his parent's vehicle and killing them. It was all just a myth—God. Nothing more, nothing less. He would keep telling himself that until the day he died.

He glanced over at the clock and groaned, realizing he was late. It was already 10:45 in the morning. He drank more than the usual amount of alcohol last night and passed out. He had yet to remember how he got into his bed.

Ethan slipped some fresh clothes on, having no time for a shower. Then, doused himself in cologne. It was the best he could do for now.

He felt guilty for even considering this woman's offer. He had almost everything he could ever want, yet he was a miserable man. He should have declined and just stuck with his usual double chocolate chip muffin. Hope was being generous though, and generosity was something he rarely received. Although, he was already ruining it by being extremely late.

He stepped out of the house his mom and dad had left in his name and began heading to Downtown Alton. Illinois was chilly this morning, and November was showing off its best today.

"Hope, would you stop pacing? Just forget it. Ethan's not going to come. He's probably too hungover to remember his own name." Brianna shoved a pan of banana bread in the oven, wincing at her harsh words.

Hope shot her sister an icy glare. Bri had a habit of not thinking before she spoke. She really needed to work on that.

"I was really praying that he would be here." She chewed on her lip. The disappointment was real. Hope had only wanted to help Ethan. It was more than just the muffins; it was about so much more.

"Maybe God had a different plan in mind. Just wait it out, Hope." Hope knew her sister meant what she said.

Wait. There was that word again. Hope half-smiled to herself. *I'll wait for you, Lord.*

She watched her sister begin to work another batch of triple-berry muffins. "You're right."

"I know." Bri smirked and quickly pulled her bleach blonde hair into a ponytail.

"Conceited much?" Hope raised an eyebrow at her sister's response.

"Never," she teased.

"Hey, can you help me carry these boxes of banana cream cupcakes out to the counter? Mark should be here any minute to pick them up." Hope politely asked.

"Sure thing, sista!" Bri sang and Hope shook her head at the notes Brianna sang off-key.

"You know you like my songs, just admit it." Hope's sister nudged her with a chuckle.

"Never," she threw back Bri's words at her.

"Touché." Both sisters laughed and walked out of the kitchen.

"What's all of this laughter for?" Dressed in a snazzy work suit, Mark walked around the counter to help them with the load of bakery boxes.

"Oh, your sister." Bri and Hope spoke in unison, accusing one another. They made eye contact and then burst into a fit of laughter. Siblings and laughter were definitely the best medicine.

"You two are crazy." Mark shook his head with a smile, probably not even wanting to know what was behind their laughter.

"But you love us," Hope added with a cheesy grin.

"That I do." Her brother poured himself a cup of coffee and took a seat on the blush pink colored barstool beside his partner, Brandon.

"How are you this morning, Brandon?" Hope decided to speak to him since Bri apparently refused.

"Lovely, now that your beautiful sister gets to see me this morning," he answered with a sly grin and winked in Bri's direction. Hope caught Bri's more than loud, very dramatic huff.

Brandon was Mark's lifetime best friend, and now his partner—deputy police chief. They grew up together going to church, playing baseball, football, hide and seek—somehow Mark would always coincidentally find Brandon hiding in Brianna's room. Brandon was always seeking for Brianna just to aggravate her, but he had a good heart. Hope prayed that the two of them would eventually become an "item." Brandon would be good for Bri. For now, though, Hope would keep her lips sealed.

"In your dreams." Bri rolled her eyes at him and disappeared back into the kitchen.

They're in love. Mark quietly and carefully mouthed the words across the counter to Hope. She bit her lip to suppress the laughter building up within her.

"How is work going this morning?" Hope asked while she poured Brandon a cup of coffee.

"This morning is slow, but last night there was a pretty bad car accident. I have yet to receive the woman's personal information, including her name. But say a prayer for her, she could use it," Mark told his sister and she nodded. Hope hated car accidents. "What about your morning with Mr. Grey?" Mark asked, referring to Ethan.

"He didn't show up." Hope instantly looked down at the floor, feeling embarrassed that her plans had fallen through.

Hope didn't try to hide her disappointment, and Mark clearly saw it. "Maybe he'll be around later." He tried to comfort her.

She half smiled, appreciating her brother. "Are you going to Mom and Dad's tomorrow for dinner before the Wednesday night church service?" She changed the subject to a tradition her family had started when her siblings all moved out on their own: A delicious Wednesday evening dinner with her mother's divine cooking skills, then they would go to church that night together as a family.

"Wouldn't miss it for the world." He smiled and stood up from his seat. "I hate to run, but the guys back at work are probably starved by now. What do I owe you?" Mark reached into the pocket of his navy uniform slacks for his wallet.

"A hug." She walked around the counter as he embraced her in a tight squeeze. His hugs were the absolute best.

"Thank you. Although, you're going in the hole with all the cupcakes you've given me for free recently." He laughed, letting her go.

Hope stood on her toes and ruffled Mark's brown hair. "When I need something, I'll let you know." She spoke with a sly grin.

"Oh, I'm sure you will." He sighed with a chuckle.

"Tell your antisocial sister that I said goodbye." Brandon winked, referring to Bri, who must have purposefully gotten lost in the kitchen.

"Of course." Hope laughed. "I'll see you boys later. Be safe." She waved them goodbye.

"It's between the triple berry muffin and the blueberry streusel muffin. This is a lifechanging decision, I hope you're aware of that." He grinned with his gaze concentrated on the two muffins, trying to make up his mind.

Ethan had shown up at the bakery at 11:30 A.M. He'd apologized for being late, but he knew Hope saw past his lame excuses. He felt ashamed of that but was thankful she didn't ask any further questions.

"Ah, good choices. You know, you could just change up your order every other day. Like a normal person." She laughed as she wiped up crumbs on the counter from the previous muffins he had sampled.

He had to admit, Hope was pretty. Her long, slick blonde hair had a tint of red to it that made her green eyes pop. After watching her work behind the counter and in and out of the kitchen many mornings, he found his favorite feature of hers, apart from her glistening smile, were her freckles. Not an excessive number of freckles, but enough to make them stand out. It reminded him of his mom. Although, she had freckles all over her. As a kid, Ethan had loved playing connect the dots with his fingers on his mom's face. He could almost hear his mom giggling as he thought about it.

Ethan shook himself from the picture. No sense in going there right now. "Being normal isn't fun though." He shrugged as he thought for a moment. Which muffin? "I know what you should do!" He made his face light up big time.

Hope smiled at his expression, apparently happy to see him brighten up. "You've got a genius idea, don't you?" she gushed.

"Because I can't decide, you should make a mixed berry streusel muffin. It would lessen my pain about having to choose between the two. One's going to feel bad if I don't pick it." He stuck out his bottom lip and looked up at her with a glimmer of hope in his eyes.

"First of all, foods don't have feelings." She laughed and he rolled his eyes with a chuckle. "Second, that's not a bad idea. It wouldn't be too hard to mush the recipes together." He watched Hope debate the idea.

"Well you said it. I *am* a genius." He emphasized the last four words.

Hope grabbed a sticky note and a pen by the register and noted his idea. "I'm going to need someone to taste test them though," she hinted at him.

"I wonder who would be willing to do that…" He pretended to think long and hard.

"I don't have time for games. Would you like to help me try them out sometime?" She sighed with a laugh.

He chuckled. She gave up so easily. Hope was more of a cut to the chase kind of person, he realized. "I'd love to. Give me a day, time, and place. I'll try my best to be on time."

"Try harder than you did this morning, okay?" Hope laughed, but her smile quickly vanished after seeing the look on his face. Ethan deserved it though, he gave her his word and hadn't followed through this morning.

"I'm sorry. I didn't mean it that way." She grimaced. "I'm going to be bruised by the many kicks I'm mentally giving myself right now."

Ethan knew that she meant the apology, but for some reason little things like that still hurt him. He tried not to let the depression show. He was pathetic, for he was at war with himself. He wanted to give up and drown in his sorrows, yet he wanted to believe in himself. He wanted others to believe in him, but he didn't feel like trying. "No harm done." He tried to shake it off with a fake smile, but he could tell that Hope didn't believe him.

"Ethan, if you ever need anything. I'm here. I'll always talk." Hope spoke softly after a few minutes of silence.

She pulled out another sticky note and scribbled down some numbers. "Call me anytime. I don't care if it's three in the morning." She managed a laugh.

He appreciated it and knew that the gesture came straight from her heart. Others had done and said the same things in the past, but never meant it. They just had pity on him. Pity that he put this quiet, peaceful town to shame.

"Thank you." He looked into her green eyes that held a sparkle in them.

She was beautiful. Not just on the outside, the inside was even better. She had a heart of gold, and she didn't even know it. Ethan saw everything he'd once wanted in Hope Lawson, but he'd never end up with a girl like her now. He might not end up with anyone.

Ethan took a deep, shaky breath and grabbed the telephone on his bedside table. He had to call his sister back, no matter how ugly their last conversation had been. Hope's concern for Ethan made him suddenly want to check on Sara himself.

He dialed the number she had last called him on. While he listened to phone ring, he seriously debated on hanging up. Sara was probably just going to give him down the road again.

Pacing in front of his bedroom window, he watched dark storm clouds huddled together in the night sky, painting a picture of how Ethan's insides felt.

She finally picked up around the fifth ring, making Ethan's heartrate pick up speed. "Hello?" To his surprise, her speech sounded groggy.

"Sara, you called earlier?" He kept his voice monotone.

She sucked in a breath that made Ethan wince. "Ethan, I've been in a car accident."

three

This couldn't be happening, not again. His chest pounded louder than his thoughts. "What happened?" Ethan asked.

He could hear his sister trying to muster the strength to speak, and he patiently waited for her to respond. "A drunk driver."

At the three spoken words, his heart plummeted. Ethan felt the whole weight of the world come crashing down on his shoulders. He didn't know what to say. *What did he say?* For some reason, he felt incredibly guilty. Ethan had driven drunk many times in the past. He had just been fortunate enough to not get caught. He'd always ended somewhere safe. It was like he was being cut down the middle again, but this time it wasn't Sara's fault. "Are you okay?" was all he could manage to get out.

"I have a gash on my forehead. It'll leave a scar. They've already stitched it up." She stammered, fumbling around with words. "I received the results to all my tests an hour ago. My neck's broken and I have a fractured ankle." Her gloomy voice spoke volumes. This wasn't the sister he once knew. Sara used to be strong-willed and positive. This accident had obviously shaken her up.

His head hung low. A fractured ankle they could deal with, a neck...well, it concerned Ethan. "How bad is your neck?"

"It could be worse. I could be unconscious or dead, but I'm not. The first few minutes after I woke up were awful. The shock was horrendous. I couldn't speak and the pain had a rippling effect, but I guess you could say I've made improvement since last night. They've even moved me into my own room, and I'm breathing on my own again."

Ethan winced at how she described everything. He should have called her back this morning. He gathered from what she'd said that the accident happened sometime late last night or early this morning.

"I can't even hold onto the phone. Sweet Clara, my nurse, put it on speaker and gave me ten minutes. I can't move. My body from the neck down is numb." She sighed and took a moment to rest before she completely lost her voice.

"Give me fifteen minutes and I'll be at the hospital." It was already 10:50 P.M. but he didn't care. Ethan's heart told him he needed to be with his sister.

She didn't protest, just softly responded, "Okay."

Twenty minutes later, he had finally arrived at the hospital. The air seemed thick, dark, and melancholy, but maybe Ethan was getting the weather confused with his emotions. Rain lightly dripped from the sky and trickled down his leather jacket.

He watched as the back of an ambulance opened and emergency medical technicians rushed to get a stretcher inside the

ER. The raised voices caused so many sentiments to bubble up inside of him. He could hear the EMT's as they shouted and tried to save his parent's lives. He could see his mom struggling for her last breath. Ethan despised the hospital with a passion. No one was ever there for a good reason. It was almost as depressing as his own life.

After asking a male secretary at the front desk where Sara was staying, he headed up to her room. His palms began to sweat profusely as his nerves built inside of him. Ethan hadn't seen his sister for quite a while because of his own selfishness.

As he raised his hand to knock on the door to her room, a nurse on the other end swung it open. "Finally, a guest!" Her smile stated she didn't mean any harm by her statement. "Come in, but please be quiet. We gave her some pain medication a few minutes ago and she drifted back to sleep," she whispered. "Poor Sara hasn't had anyone here for her since the wreck yesterday evening."

Ethan felt a pang of responsibility settle on his shoulders. After all, he was Sara's one and only brother and he was supposed to be there for her, yet he had failed immensely. "I'm her brother." He half-smiled as the nurse held out her hand to greet him.

"I'm Clara, Sara's nurse. I've been working around the clock to take care of this sweet girl." The nurse was older, but she seemed genuine, and he found no judgment in her eyes.

"I appreciate that." He diverted his attention to his sister lying on the hospital bed with beeping machines surrounding her. "How's she doing?"

Sara looked uncomfortable on the long hospital bed that probably felt like cement. He stared at the brace around her neck and winced. Ethan wanted to run the other direction, but he kept his feet firmly planted on the ugly green tile floor. Sara's long brown hair was sloppily pinned up in a messy bun. He knew if his sister could see herself, the most of her worries would be about her hairstyle. If she put her hair up, it was always neat and slick, never a mess.

Even as she slept, Ethan could sense the pain she felt. The facial expression settled on her face spoke volumes.

"She's lucky to be alive. I'm surprised that she's doing as well as she is already. Typically, she wouldn't even be talking at this point, but she's trying and succeeding, which is a huge sign of improvement." The nurse sighed and continued to explain. "Now she does have what we would call temporary paralysis. With her being as young as she is and already doing as well as she is, she will fully recover from that in no time.

"The neck though, it's going to take quite a while. Her doctor is preparing her for surgery in a couple hours, then physical therapy until she gets back to normal."

He cringed. "She's going to hate that." Sara's strong-willed nature always kept her accomplishing things by herself, hardly ever accepting help.

The nurse proceeded to finish. "I wouldn't be worried about her fractured ankle, it's tightly wrapped, but only a minor fracture. It will cause getting back to her feet a little more difficult, but again, it's the last thing you need to worry about.

"The gash on her forehead is bandaged and stitched up, the most it will do is cause some headaches. The whole situation is no fun. She'll have to cope to diverse ways than she's used to." Clara paused. "Sir, you're very blessed that your sister is alive. If I were in your shoes, I'd be on my knees thanking God. He's performed miracles on Sara already. I truly believe that she wouldn't be doing this well if it wasn't for Him. He kept His hand over her."

Ethan hadn't thought about God. He hadn't had time. If God were real, his sister wouldn't be sitting in the hospital dealing with excruciating pain right now. He just simply gave the nurse a small smile, not wanting to argue with her.

After excusing herself, Clara stepped out of the room to give Ethan some time alone with his sister. He took a seat in an uncomfortable black leather chair beside of his sister's bed. The beeping noises all over the room were still running smoothly, and he found himself thankful for that.

He gingerly picked up Sara's dainty hand and rubbed the back of it with his thumb. The realization hit him like a ton of bricks, Ethan was the one that had let their bond fall apart. They had been each other's best friends—inseparable—until he had let alcohol come between them and ruin their relationship. He had selfishly thought, after their mom and dad's passing, that he was the only one hurting. That the pain was his to bear. He never took consideration of his sister's emotions and what she was going through.

The guilt about being alone and not having anyone there for him for so long pressed on his shoulders. It was all his fault. The decision to shove his sister out of the way three years ago had been a wrong one. He realized then that he had wasted so much time only thinking of himself. *Selfish.* He could have had someone there for him all this time, but he'd pushed Sara away.

Why had it taken him this long to realize it?

"I'm sorry," was all he could whisper.

Sara needed a brother, and starting right now, he was going to try to be a better one… no matter how much sacrificing it took.

She opened the back of the delivery van and Anne, Brianna, and Mark started carrying several boxes of cupcakes. Catering the desserts to weddings was one of Hope's favorite things about running a bakery. She was thankful Mark volunteered to help them on his day off duty. She had to admit that if her business was going to stay this busy, she was going to have to hire more staff. She never dreamed people would love Funfetti Café and Bakery this much. She thanked God for the business and for fulfilling parts of her dreams.

The reception area was an immense enclosed pavilion with a lake and field for its scenery. The pavilion didn't even seem like it was enclosed. There were so many windows and so much space. It was like a fairytale that made Hope's jaw drop as she walked in. Everything was stunning. Lights were strung everywhere, along with colorful tulle wrapped around many balloons. The Hammons had picked a perfect location for their reception.

"Oh, my stars! This is gorgeous." Brianna sat a tray of cupcakes on a table and took in her surroundings.

"It's perfect!" Hope glanced around the room for the cake display table. It looked like the caterers for dinner were here and possibly a wedding planner, she assumed as she saw a woman dressed in slick black pants with her hair perfectly pinned away from her face, heading toward them. She carried a clipboard and held her nose high in the air.

"We're here with the desserts. I'm Hope, and these are my assistants." Hope smiled and introduced everyone.

"Nice to meet you, Madame. I'm Adalene. If you follow me, I'll show you where you may display the cakes." The wedding planner's French accent made her even more professional. Hope already knew that Brianna envied Adalene, Bri had always wanted an accent.

Beside of the bride and groom's table was a table decorated especially for the cakes. There were labels already in place for the assorted flavors of the cupcakes, and a large golden stand for the cake in the center. Hope expressed her thanks to Adalene, who was already a step ahead of Hope. It shrugged away less stress on Hope's own shoulders.

After showing them around, Adalene ran off to make sure there were enough flowers for each table. The woman definitely had more patience than Hope.

"Let's get to putting the cupcakes on their stands, shall we?" Anne clapped her hands together and opened a box of cupcakes.

"Mark, can you help me get the wedding cake out of the van?" He only nodded and followed Hope like a lost puppy in unfamiliar territory. Bless his heart. They left Anne and Bri to start displaying cupcakes.

They stepped out into the fresh, yet chilly air. The breeze tossed Hope's long hair back and forth as it blew. Almost a week had passed, and she had heard nothing from Ethan. She hadn't even seen him linger around her shop. She was beginning to get worried about him. Was it something she said that he didn't like? Maybe she shouldn't have given him her phone number, but she thought it was a nice, genuine offer. Hope didn't like questioning herself, especially when she thought she initially did the right thing.

She decided to change the subject on her mind by talking to her brother. "Thank

44

you for coming on your day off. I really appreciate it."

"It's the least I could do, considering I basically steal your cupcakes most of the time." He opened the back of the van.

Hope smiled, he'd do anything for her and she knew it. "How has work been this week?"

"Yesterday, there was a shooting at the mall." He shook his head. "It was ugly, there were injuries but luckily no one died. The worst part was that the shooter killed himself." Hope watched in awe as her brave brother spoke of this as if it were normal.

Being police chief came with a price. Hope always feared that one day he'd get himself into an even bigger situation. One where she wouldn't be able to do anything but pray.

She picked up the edge of the wedding cake as Mark grabbed the other end. "I don't know what I'd do without prayer." She sighed, knowing that without prayer, her life and the people around her would crumble. "Speaking of prayer, I've been praying for the girl that was in the car accident. Did you ever get a name?" she asked, curiosity getting the best of her.

"Sorry, I meant to tell you. Her name was Sara Grey. They said she broke her neck and fractured her ankle. The drunk driver died."

Hope stopped in her tracks, almost dropping the cake in her hands. "Grey? Does Ethan Grey have any siblings?"

Mark cocked his head sideways and squinted his eyes—his thinking face. Hope wanted to laugh at her brother's thought process procedure, but she kept it to herself. Mark had probably been too busy to even think about Sara's accident, he had bigger cases to work. It made sense though. She couldn't think of any other Grey's that lived in Alton.

Hope knew the way her brother thought, he was worried about her getting involved with Ethan. Being a cop, he saw the ugly side to every situation. He wouldn't want her to get hurt. But also, being a minister called by God, he would understand her deep desire to help and share God's love with others. She knew her brother like the back of her hand.

"It makes sense. You haven't talked to him in a week, and it's almost made a week since the accident." He clicked his tongue.

"He must not have known about it when he came in the day after." Hope took a shot in the dark.

"I can give Brandon a call once I'm free and he could check it out for me if you'd like," he offered. He probably knew that if he didn't do something about it, Hope would just find out for herself.

"That'd be great." She let the gratitude show.

"Now, we have a wedding to cater to, my little lobster." Mark grinned at the nickname that would never die. They started carefully walking the cake to the reception area.

If she didn't have a cake in her hand, she would've whacked him. "I will take my whisk and beat you to a pulp," Hope threatened.

"Not that intimidating." Mark smirked at her threat.

47

Many hours later, a shower, and change into comfy clothes, Hope finally plopped down onto her couch. While weddings were her favorite, they were exhausting. The bride was ecstatic when she saw the cake. The word *perfect* rolled off her tongue more than once. Hope smiled to herself. It couldn't have gone any better.

On the car ride back with her siblings and Anne, they officially decided to hire more staff. At least two more people to help in the kitchen and two or three more to help in the café. After this weekend was over, she already had orders for two birthdays and one anniversary. She needed more help for her growing business.

Hope and her sister, Brianna, started with a small dream as little kids. Their parents fully supported them, and they went after it. After two years in culinary school for Hope and waiting for her sister to graduate and take classes herself, they took out a loan and bought a building. Introducing Funfetti Café and Bakery to the world. Hope honestly didn't know how the bakery had received this much publicity. It was amazing to look at where they started versus where they were at now. It was a blessing from God, was the only explanation.

She headed to the kitchen with a blanket snuggly wrapped around her shoulders. The weather had her craving a hot chocolate. November was settling in, and before long it would be winter. She loved this time of year—baking the pumpkin pie cupcakes, drinking hot chocolate, and being with family even more than the usual. And of course, the cheesy Christmas romance movies that even her brother secretly liked.

She grabbed a mug with a hand drawn turkey on the front of it. It had been given to her as a gift a year ago from a preschooler that she taught in Sunday Bible class. Teaching the youth was something she loved doing. Kids made her happy to be around, and she loved reading and teaching them the accounts recorded in the Bible. Although many of the kids were ornery, she couldn't help but admire them. They always seemed ecstatic for a new lesson and craft.

Once her hot chocolate was made, she headed back to the living room to watch a movie. As she sat her mug full of marshmallows and cocoa on the marbled end table, her phone rang. She picked it up and read the caller ID. Mark.

"What's up, big bro?" she answered, wishing she had an annoying nickname for him.

She placed him on speaker as she sat down on the couch. "Hey, I just got off the phone with Brandon." He sighed. "Ethan indeed does have a sister, and it's Sara."

Hope hung her head low. Ethan's sister *had* been in a car accident.

"Apparently he's been at the hospital by her side ever since he heard the news. That's surprising seeing how hungover and depressed he's been lately." Her brother filled her in on all the details.

"Maybe this could be an eyeopener." Hope bit her lip, a habit she often made when she was nervous. She prayed that this situation could open Ethan's eyes. He needed Christ in his life. He needed hope beyond life's problems.

"Maybe so. From what Brandon got out of the doctors, she's made tremendous improvement. She had temporary paralysis, but she's recovering from that. Her nurse said that she came out of surgery for her neck well. She has lots of physical therapy time once she recovers from the surgery," Mark informed her. "Being a brother to sisters automatically places you a role as a protector. Maybe this will cause Ethan to see it's time to step up and be one." He added a glimmer of hope.

Hope treasured the last two sentences of Mark's. She truly appreciated him. "Do they have any other family in the state?" she asked curiously.

Hope could hear her brother mutter something but couldn't place what he'd said. "Could you speak louder?" she requested.

Mark took a deep breath. Hope didn't understand what was taking him forever. "Three years ago, they lost both of their parents in a very brutal car accident. They took a hit by a semi. I guess I could see why he lives the way he does. To him, it seems like no one's there for him. So, he's drowning his life in alcohol as an excuse to forget everything. I told you, *everyone* has a reason behind their ways. I believe this is his."

Three years. He'd been a drunk for three years. He'd visited the bakery for almost three years, and Hope didn't even know half of the man's story. Hope couldn't believe it. She couldn't imagine losing her own parents, especially the way Ethan had. Her family, along with God of course, was her life. Losing them would be like losing an enormous chunk of life. It'd never be the same. "That's awful, I couldn't even imagine it."

"Neither could I," Mark's melancholy voice whispered.

"What hospital is Sara staying at?"

"The local one. Downtown." He paused. "You're planning on visiting, aren't you?" She could almost hear his smile through the way he worded the question.

"I wouldn't have it any other way." A smile formed on her own face.

"Do you need someone to come with you?" Mark was already offering to do something else for her, and she chuckled.

"Haven't you done enough already? Besides, I'm going to have Bri go with me tomorrow."

"Does she have plans for tomorrow?" he asked, amused.

"She does now." Hope laughed. It didn't matter what, she was always volunteering her sister for something. "So, I should probably get off the phone and warn her. Thanks for this."

He laughed. "She'll do anything for her precious older sister, and apparently so will I. Even if I am the oldest. Seems like I need to stand my ground." He caused her to laugh. "Goodnight, Hope."

"Goodnight, Bub," she sang as she hung up the cell phone.

Hope found herself feeling more than relieved at the discovery that Ethan wasn't just ignoring her, but she felt terrible that his sister was hurt, and Hope had a feeling so was he. Maybe not physically but hurt mentally and spiritually.

Hope took a sip of her cocoa and dialed her sister's phone number. Bri picked up after the third ring.

"Hello?"

FINDING HOPE

"I need you to be at my house in less than fifteen minutes. Pronto!" And with that, Hope hung up the phone.

four

Did you fill the coffee thermos?" Hope asked whilst she checked her pockets for keys.

Bri and Hope had stayed up most of the night to come up with the perfect recipe for mixed berry streusel muffins. After three batches were tossed, they finally resulted with a fabulous blend of triple berry and blueberry streusel muffins.

"Yes, and the creamer is inside of the bag," her sister called from Hope's closet.

"Hope, I'm borrowing one of your sweaters. Seeing how you called me last night and I had no clue what was going on, you owe it to me. My current shirt is covered in streusel crumbs and flour." Brianna blamed her sister.

When Brianna finally made it to Hope's apartment last night, she had mistaken Hope's urgent request for her as a serious emergency. When Hope explained that she wanted to personally gift Ethan and Sara muffins, Bri nearly socked Hope in the face. Hope had to apologize for being so hasty and scaring the life out of her little sister. Though, once she fully explained Ethan's situation to Bri, Brianna completely understood and was more than happy to help Hope. They had worked so hard last night that they ended up crashing in the living room after their baking success. Hope considered the two of them a team.

Brianna strolled into the kitchen to help Hope gather the muffins and coffee. Bri had picked out a blush pink, loosely knit sweater to wear. Hope's favorite sweater.

"Don't ruin that." Hope pointed to the sweater on her sister's body. Although, she had to admit, it looked good on Brianna. It suited her petite, slender body. She wore two thick braids parted down both sides of her head which made the outfit even cuter.

"You mean...don't do this?" Brianna teased her sister by bringing the coffee thermos up to her sweater and tilting it ever so slightly without spilling anything. She laughed as she watched Hope's eyes bulge out of her head.

Hope swatted Brianna's arm. "I will run over your favorite pair of shoes if you don't put a lid on that coffee." She referred to Bri's black and white Converse. Hope was going to buy her sister a new pair for Christmas. Bri's old ones were disgusting and falling apart at the soles.

"You wouldn't dare kill a fly, let alone run over my favorite pair of shoes," Bri pointed out with a snicker.

"Grab your coat." Hope held back a smile, attempting to distract her sister. She knew it was true, but she wasn't going to willingly admit to the fact. "Now, let's get out of here." She shut the door and headed toward her car.

It was a surprisingly warm day for November. The wind was blowing gently, but the air was a perfect temperature of seventy degrees. With the crisp brown leaves falling from the trees, it looked like the world was covered in a cobbler crust of brown sugar and cinnamon. She watched her neighbor's three-year-old jump into a pile of leaves, and she giggled as she shut her car door. *Oh, to be a kid again.*

"So, is there any other reason you're visiting Ethan and Sara, other than the fact that she's been in an accident?" Brianna clicked her seatbelt into place as Hope started driving.

Hope knew exactly what her sister was hinting at. She'd already mentally prepared herself for Bri's flippant questions. "Can't a person just show some empathy for others?"

"You're not the least bit interested in him?" Brianna narrowed her eyes down to slits.

"Bri, he's an alcoholic. He probably doesn't even care to know about God. Plus, I don't know much about him. He's quite the opposite of what I look for in a guy." Hope paused as she made a right onto a busy street. Part of what she'd said was true, but maybe she was *attracted* to him. Not interested, though. "I'm just trying to do something nice. I'd like to show him that someone cares for him. Actions speak louder than words."

Bri nodded, finally getting the hint. "I'm your sister. I'm supposed to be curious." She answered the look of on Hope's face.

Hope smiled. Her sister was always full of curiosity. It had always been a challenge keeping a secret from her. Brianna would detect the slightest change in mood and instantly have a million questions to ask. Hope found it good for their relationship though. Bri always made it clear she never wanted Hope to feel like there wasn't a time she couldn't talk to her.

"Remember that when it's vice versa." Hope glanced at her sister in the passenger's seat.

"You brought coffee *and* muffins?" Ethan's face was like a child's this morning. Even if he hadn't had rest in a week, he looked immensely well.

He placed the bright bouquet of daisies and white roses on Sara's bedside table and sat back down by a large window overlooking the river. Bri and Hope had made a pitstop to purchase flowers. Their mother had always taught them that they could never be too kind, and Hope planned on carrying out that instruction.

"I did indeed, and those specific muffins are going to be your new favorite." Hope grinned and took a seat beside Ethan.

Glancing across the cramped hospital room, Hope cringed. Sara slept in her bed; her body as stiff as a board. No way to move around and get comfortable. Her facial expressions even in her sleep told Hope just how miserable of a condition Sara was most likely in.

"Are these mixed berry streusels?" Ethan opened the lid as he grinned back at her. A smile Hope never knew he had; crinkles even met at the corner of his lips.

"She made three batches. The fourth time was a charm. You ought to feel special."

Bri leaned against the light-yellow colored wall and took a sip of her coffee.

"I really do appreciate it, and for you guys visiting. I'll make for sure to save Sara at least one. When she's feeling up to it of course." He winked in a teasing manner as he grabbed one for himself and sat the box down on the counter.

"How is she doing?" Brianna asked as she peered Sara's direction.

He sighed, taking a glance of his own at his sister. A look of concern mixed with sadness washed over his face. "The neck fusion surgery, which was earlier this week, helped the pressure of her nerves settle, but not completely yet. Her doctor is hoping to send her home tomorrow, depending on how well she feels.

"She's been walking a lot better. Her fractured ankle is healing. The paralysis is going to wear off in time, especially with physical therapy three times a week." He snorted. "She's going to love that.

"Pain is definitely a thing. Pounding headaches, nerves twitching, moving her head or shoulders, movement in general. But

I think her nightmares are the worst." He stared at the floor with a deep concentration. "She's woke up the past four nights, screaming and breaking out in sweats. I've had to call nurses to help me get her calmed down. Once she finally is awake, going back to sleep is out of the question. So, I just sit there and talk to her until that image of the accident leaves her head."

"That's awful." Hope lowered her head and twiddled her thumbs back and forth. Sara would be scarred for life with the memory of her car accident. The fact her parents died in a car crash wouldn't ease any of the pain, it would just make her even more tense.

She couldn't help but wonder if Sara was a Christian. It would make the whole situation more comforting, to know God had His hand on her.

"She's a trouper though." Ethan smiled, reassuring Hope and her sister.

Hope was finally discovering another side of Ethan. A side that she believed was the real Ethan. It was the exact opposite of seeing him hungover and miserable in the bakery. He seemed to be a gentle, positive, sweet, and caring person when he chose to be. It made her want him to come out of that low state of life he was living in and be the person God designed him to be in the first place.

She smiled back at him and took a sip of the tea that she brought with her.

"One more. Please!" Hope begged. She'd been telling Ethan jokes for the past ten minutes. Seemed like this woman didn't know a stranger. She was incredibly outgoing. It seemed to be a good distraction for the time being. She had told him telling jokes was a hobby that both her and her brother picked up to annoy and humor one another.

"One more. They're getting cheesier as they go." Ethan laughed at her enthusiasm.

"Mark enjoys my jokes." She stuck her tongue out at him.

Ethan laughed. "Believe me, I'm enjoying it." They both continued to walk. Ethan had sporadically asked Hope if she would join him on a walk. He needed fresh air and time to breathe, the hospital room was getting more stifling by the minute. Hope had agreed to a short walk while Bri generously offered to stay back and keep an eye on Sara. Sara had still been asleep when they left.

"Knock knock,"

"Who's there?" A smirk formed across Ethan's lips.

"Little old lady."

Because of his sister's personality, he had heard this joke a million times, but instead of ruining the moment for Hope, he humored her. "Little old lady who?"

"I didn't know you could yodel." Ethan was glad he let Hope finish it out. The satisfaction on her face was priceless. "Thank you everyone, thank you." She bowed three times.

She was cute…and caring too. Ethan knew Hope Lawson was kind, but not this generous. It was sweet of her to even think of him, but he was probably ruining her reputation as they spoke. *Pastor's sister hanging out with town drunk.* He could practically see the older women of Alton starting rumors now. He mentally rolled his eyes and engaged himself back into the conversation. "Baking is your thing, but jokes are not your forte," he teased, and it earned him a shove in the side of the ribs.

He laughed. "Speaking of baking, I'm sorry I never called. Things have been complicated the past week." He apologized. To be fair, he had thought about calling Hope but had decided not to. He didn't desire the extra attention.

"Honestly, it's okay. We can always bake some other time." She looked up from the pavement they had been walking on outside of the hospital.

His eyes lit up, for she was offering again, something people rarely did for him. "I would love that," he answered sincerely.

They started another lap around the hospital grounds.

"Ethan, can I ask you a question?" Hope crunched a leaf as they walked. She kept her eyes glued to the ground, avoiding eye contact.

Ethan knew from the way she was acting it was going to be a personal question, but he let her ask anyway. "Of course."

"You don't have to answer if you feel it's too personal." She paused before continuing. Hope looked up to see any sign of recognition on his face, but he just nodded, allowing her to proceed. "When did you start drinking?"

Ethan should have seen the question coming. He wondered what sparked the curiosity behind those green eyes. He drew a deep breath and answered her. "Two and a half years ago."

"What's your reasoning?"

"To forget about reality." He was honest with her but didn't go into detail. Little did he know that she already knew so much about him.

She nodded, and Ethan appreciated that she didn't ask any other questions. Tense wasn't even the right word to describe how such topics about himself made him feel. She deserved to know, but he couldn't bring himself to willingly open up fully to her. At least not yet.

"Enough about me, tell me about you." He hoped that would end the topic.

A breeze blew, and Ethan watched as cold bumps cascaded down Hope's arm. If he had a jacket, this is where he'd loan it to her. It was common courtesy. Unfortunately, he had left it back in the hospital room.

"What do you want to know?" she asked, looking up into his eyes. *Oh, those emerald eyes of hers.* Ethan found nothing but honesty looking back into his eyes.

"Tell me about your family. You seem close." He glanced at her and saw a smile as wide as the Nile River spread across her face. Just the thought of her family obviously made her happy. Maybe that was how he was supposed to feel about Sara…the *only* family member he knew.

"I have one older brother, Mark. He's a police chief and the pastor at one of our community churches. Then there's my younger sister, Bri. She's the spoiled one out of the family. You probably know what that's like. The youngest are always the babies." She mischievously grinned, causing him to laugh. Ethan playfully elbowed her side for the comment she made.

"My parents are missionaries. I don't get to see them as often as I'd like to, but what they do is amazing. I've only been on a few mission trips, but they changed my perspective on life. The word *blessed* became more special in my life once I got back to the states safely." She ran a finger through her slightly curled hair today. "Have you ever been on a mission trip?"

The memories for him started to flood back, and they hit him like a boulder. "Once, our local church went on one. My mom and dad surprised Sara and I by taking us with them. We had been begging to go on one anyway. I remember coming home and thanking God I had a shower and a bed. I told Mom and Dad I'd never take those things for granted again. One week later, I was refusing to take a shower." Ethan paused. "Mind you, I was only a kid." They both laughed.

The memories of his family were something no one could take from him, yet they stung every time he thought about them. His heart constantly ached at the fact that he couldn't just talk to his parents one last time. That he couldn't just go back in time and make things different.

They walked a little bit longer in silence, Hope giving him the time he needed.

Ethan was grateful that this girl was curious enough to check on him and sweet enough to stick around. What had been a long week, made this moment special. He'd never forget Hope and the fact that she stuck to her word. It had been something he wasn't used to. He actually felt the sincerity in her words and actions.

"Ethan, can I ask one more question?" She broke the silence.

His heart pounded. Ethan wasn't ready for any more questions. What feared him the most was opening up and letting someone back into his life again. He'd lose her for sure. Although for some reason, he nodded and let her speak anyway. It was like his body didn't function properly when he was around Hope.

"Do you still believe in God?" Her mysterious eyes searched for some sort of reflection of hope in his, but he didn't have any to offer her.

He didn't want to disappoint her, but he also didn't want to start off what could possibly be a good friendship, with a lie. He shook his head. "If God were real, he would have saved my parents from a horrific car accident. They'd still be here today." He didn't mean to sound cold, but from the look on Hope's face, he came across that way. She just looked straight ahead of her as they approached the hospital doors again. "I didn't mean to sound rude or disappoint you. I was just being honest." He *knew* he had hurt her with his words, but she played being okay well.

"It's okay. You're entitled to your own opinion." She tried to put on a smile. The smile appeared truthful, but a glimmer of disappointment was still clearly shown across her face. "And Ethan?"

"Hm?" he murmured, not paying much attention anymore. He felt like a failure from the inside out. He'd sucked the life out of himself and he didn't want to do the same thing to Hope. She was such an optimistic, life-giving woman.

"I'm really sorry about your parents." Ethan could almost see the hurt he'd held in his heart for the past three years, reflect on her face.

He shook his head and kicked a loose gravel. "You'd think I'd be used to not having them anymore. That I'd get over it.

Instead, I think each day it gets worse." He stopped walking and turned to face Hope.

She looked him dead in the eyes. "Everyone goes through grief, and everyone's process through it is different." The compassion he witnessed and heard made his heart tingle inside. Something he hadn't felt in a long time.

"Thank you." He meant it. He watched a shiver run down Hope's spine and realized it was probably time to head in. "Let's head inside. Both of our sisters have probably eaten all the muffins." They both chuckled as he nudged her along.

Hope stepped out of the dimly lit elevator and walked toward Sara's room.

Disappointed was an understatement, but she wasn't going to let the obstacle that Satan threw get in her way. If Ethan allowed her, Hope planned on being a trusted friend he could rely on. It was going to be tough to get Ethan to believe in the one and only God that he used to put so much faith and trust in. Ethan had logical reasons to be in a state of

71

unbelief. There were so many questions left unanswered. And he still wasn't telling Hope something, she had decided that when he spoke so little about his life. There was more to this guy to figure out.

God, I met this person for a reason. You've opened a door. He needs hope, and he needs a friend. Most importantly he needs You. He hasn't let anyone get close in his life for three years. He's alone and hurt. Allow me to be a friend, but also allow me to be a light. He needs You, God. I plan on being there for Him, so give me the strength and the words. Most of all, help me to do Your will.

She rounded the corner to Sara's private room. Ethan had moseyed his way downstairs to the cafeteria to bring Sara back dinner, and Hope went on to check on their sisters.

"There you are! I thought you got lost or something," Bri teased as Hope walked into Sara's room.

Sara was now wide awake, and it seemed her and Bri were getting along just fine. Sara's chestnut hair was braided, and it looked like Bri had applied some makeup on her too, even though Sara had a gorgeous face that didn't need it.

Hope met Sara's eyes and kindly smiled. "I'm Hope. It's so nice to meet you." She reached down gently to give Sara a hug.

Sara had an exquisite smile, and her blue eyes were sparkling, considering the condition she was in. "You're Brianna's sister, right? The muffin maker." Her voice was stronger than Hope had expected.

Hope laughed. "Whatever my sister told you about me is probably not true," she pestered as Brianna stuck out her tongue.

Sara rested her head back on a pillow that looked as hard as the first batch of muffins her and Brianna had burned last night. "I'm sorry you had to meet me in this condition." She sighed.

"If it wasn't for the condition you were in, you wouldn't have met me." Hope teased with a giggle, trying to lighten Sara's mood. She smiled when she saw that she succeeded.

"How are you doing?" Hope slid into the chair beside of Sara's bed.

"There are perks to being a doctor in a division of this hospital. I'm getting special treatment. So, to answer your question, I'm doing fine." She formed her lips into an attempted smile.

Hope chuckled.

After a few minutes of rest, Sara spoke again. "Hope, your brother, Chief Mark Lawson, was there when the police and ambulance arrived. I was telling Bri earlier, I remember hearing him pray." Sara let a tear fall down her face. "He asked God to keep me safe and keep me alive."

"God did just that," Hope reassured her with a smile. Seemed like Mark never failed to do the right thing. He wore the same face throughout every day of his life that he did behind the pulpit on Sunday's. "A little spoken prayer can go a long way."

Sara wetted her lips, getting herself ready to speak more. "Hope, I selfishly walked out on God when my parents passed. Ethan and I fought like cats and dogs after that, and I didn't understand that God even had a plan through my pain. I still don't understand it all but getting so close to death has shaken me up. I remember having such a

74

peace with God at one point in my life. I lost it, and now I desperately want it back." She shifted from the position in her bed, sniffling. "How do I get back to the place I was at before the mess?"

Sara longed for God's presence in her life, Hope could plainly see it. "Sara, the hardest part is over. You have realized that you are not perfect. *Everyone* makes mistakes. All you must do is ask God to forgive you, and He will do just that. His grace, love, and mercy cover a multitude of sin. He loves you, and He wants to be your Protector." Hope grabbed Sara's hand, hoping it would give her some comfort. "If you want to go back to the place of true peace and joy, just believe in Him and accept Him."

Hope watched as wet tears flowed down Sara's cheeks. She silently prayed that Sara would trust in God once again. Sara would have a peace settled in her life, and God wouldn't let her down, even when storms would arrive. It just may spark a new hope in Ethan's life as well.

She'd let God guide her through her words, now it was time to watch Him work through Sara's decision.

After a few minutes of silence and tears, Sara spoke, but barely above a whisper. "Hope, would you and Bri pray with me? I want my peace back." Tears flowed down her cheeks, causing a few salty tears to fall from Hope's own eyes.

"That's what friends are for." Bri beamed as she made her way to the other side of Sara's bed.

The three of them grabbed hands and went into a Holy Spirit filled prayer. Hope could feel God's very presence even in a dingy hospital room. Praise God for muffins and Jesus's love that still attracted millions.

five

"**W**ould you like for me to pick up some coffee at the café? Maybe some cupcakes?" Ethan offered, keeping his eyes on the road in front of him.

Sara had officially been released from the hospital Monday afternoon. It had been a fight just getting her in the truck with him. She feared getting back inside a vehicle, that the same thing would happen again. However, after convincing her he'd only go sixty miles per hour in the slow lane on the interstate and that he'd fix her dinner, she finally got situated in his truck. He could tell by the way she gripped her seat and squeezed her eyes shut that she wasn't comfortable.

She had many restrictions for a few months that Ethan knew she wouldn't like. Especially not going back to work. She was a well-respected doctor in the hospital with crazy hours assisting, and helping others recover. It was her job, and Ethan understood she was passionate about it.

Nonetheless, Sara was ready to go home with no more monitors attached to her, and to sleep in her personal bed. She'd stated that over and over in Ethan's ear. He had realized when the doctor released her that he was going to have to stay with her until she could do things on her own. There was no way he was leaving her stranded after all she had gone through this past week.

"Plain chocolate, with white icing." Sara reclined back into the passenger seat carefully.

Ethan smiled to himself. His sister had never been the adventurous type when it came to trying new things. For as long as he could remember her favorite dessert had always been chocolate cake and vanilla icing. She hadn't changed one bit. Maybe that's where he got his consistency from. "Nothing new?"

"I said chocolate and white icing. Not a pineapple upside down cupcake with piña colada icing."

She was moody. Ethan discovered earlier in the week that it had been the pain killers that made her snarky. Sara woke up from a nap a few days ago dehydrated, and practically snapped at him for not getting ice fast enough.

He laughed. "Chocolate it is."

"Don't you dare forget the white icing." She held up her pointer finger for him to see.

"You mean vanilla?" He smirked, trying to aggravate her.

"White. There's a difference." She narrowed her brows as if he were supposed to know these things.

He laughed and then called in their order at Hope's bakery. Ethan watched Sara close her eyes again as he drove. He missed this. The endless banter, yet the boundless sibling love they had for one another. It was like nothing had changed, but in reality…everything had.

"Ethan?" She opened her eyes again long enough to look at him.

"Hmm?"

"Once I get back on my feet again, I'm going to start going back to church."

He almost slammed on the brakes at Sara's rather bold statement, but he caught himself before he did. "Why?" He didn't understand why she would want to. God *wasn't* real.

"Coming so close to death was frightening. But if I close my eyes, I can still hear the prayer of that police chief. He asked God to keep me alive and safe. He cared so much, and he didn't even know me. I remember opening my eyes for just a second to see the tears cascade down his face, then there was darkness. In that moment of darkness, I thought it was over with. I thought surely my life had ended." She took a deep breath, and Ethan looked over to see a tear escape her eye.

For a moment, a breathtaking chill shivered down his spine. Reality wanted to slap him in the face at Sara's last sentence. Death was a frigid word that made his numb soul shudder.

"When I woke up," Sara continued, "I remembered thinking it was a second chance. I can't mess this one up, Ethan. I asked God to forgive me, and I feel at peace again. For so long, I was furious with God for ripping our parents out of our lives, but Hope showed me a Bible verse yesterday to ponder on in the book of Isaiah. It says, '*my thoughts are not your thoughts, neither are your ways my ways, saith the Lord.*' Ethan, I don't understand why God took our parents to Heaven early on in our adulthood. I don't think I ever will, but I have to trust that His ways are better than mine."

Ethan didn't understand. They both trusted in God once and He hadn't answered their prayers. What made her think He would answer them this time? "He's just going to let you down again. I don't want to see you get hurt by something that isn't real." He spoke too soon and mentally cursed at himself.

She smiled at him. *Why was she smiling?* "You'll come to your senses soon enough, bub. God's not going to let me down. Man might, but God will not."

He gripped the steering wheel harder. He didn't want to blow up on her, tell her that this was preposterous, so he squeezed the wheel until his knuckles turned pale. It was the only way to keep his roller coaster of emotions from spilling out on her.

"Your fingers are going to fall off if you don't quit constricting that wheel." She laughed. "Look, no matter if you choose to believe that Jesus Christ is the Son of God, and that He is in Heaven with His Father right now, I'll still be your sister, and I'll still be here for you. I just pray you would consider it again."

Three people in the past week had mentioned God to him. First the nurse, then Hope, and now his sister. He didn't want to talk about it. He chose to believe that after all those years obeying God, only for God to not answer his prayer when his parents were lying in hospital beds dying, God simply wasn't real. God said in the Bible that He loved those who followed Him and would answer their prayers. Yet, God never answered the one prayer that Ethan needed to be answered most in his life.

Since Sara was in pain, he wasn't going to argue any further. He sighed. "And I'm your brother."

Sara chewed on her lip, something that made Ethan nauseated. *What was his sister thinking about?* "I'm glad that you mentioned that. I was wondering if you'd do something for me."

Her plans and favors were always well thought out. Ethan never liked them. They always tended to involve too much work. "Anything for you, dearest Sara." Sarcasm flew out of his mouth. It was a language they both spoke too well.

"You said so yourself." She paused with a grin. "I start physical therapy tomorrow. You're going to visit Pastor Mark tomorrow. It's just a block away, and you have to drop me off anyway."

"No." He didn't even know the reason why, but he didn't want to go.

"Hear me out. You haven't had a sip of alcohol since you came to the hospital.

You've been by my side twenty-four seven. So, basically an entire week, right?"

He didn't realize that. Ethan had been sober for a week. The more the thoughts reeled in his mind, the more his tongue desired a drip of the poison. It would relieve all his stress from the past week. He'd been thinking too much recently, and it was doing things to his heart. Things that Ethan didn't want to face. "Right," he acknowledged between gritted teeth.

"Ethan, you have improved so much in a week. You seem happier, and livelier. Why not go talk to Mark Lawson? He's proved to help more than five alcoholics in our little city overcome their addiction recently," she said. "You don't even have to talk about the Bible and Christianity with him if you're not ready for that. I'd just really like for you to talk about your addiction with him. He'll give you room to speak." She didn't give *him* time to speak though. "Ethan, knowing you were out there, the possibility of you getting hurt, and me not knowing anything for the past three years, it's terrified me. I apologize for the things I've said to you that were rude and uncalled for. I'm your older sister, I should've been there for you."

84

"Only by three years." He pointed out their age difference, not ready to recognize anything else she'd mentioned. Sara was twenty-eight and Ethan was twenty-five. "Even if you are older, I am the brother. I should've been the man. Should have been there by your side, catching the tears." The guilt still resided on his shoulders.

"I don't want to go back to the way it was, me and you fighting constantly. I'm ashamed of that. I just want to try to repair our relationship as brother and sister. It's what Mom and Dad would want." She shifted in the passenger seat to make herself semi-comfortable.

"I agree." His parents would have never wanted this. When Sara and Ethan fought as kids, their mom and dad would immediately have them make up. They would always remind them that they were siblings, they were supposed to be the best of friends. His bottom lip trembled at thought of his parent's wise words. Ethan was letting his mom and dad down.

"Will you give it a try? One day is all I'm asking for," she asked, hoping.

He rubbed his lip with his thumb and sighed. "I'm not saying no, and I'm not saying yes, yet. Give me some time to think, okay?"

"That's all I'm asking for." Sara closed her eyes with a satisfied smile skewed across her face.

Surely talking to Mark Lawson one time wouldn't hurt. Do for family, right?

six

He was going to hate this. He was only doing it for his sister. Hopefully after today she would drop the subject for good. Stepping foot back into a church made Ethan's stomach queasy. The last time he had been in a church was at his mom and dad's funeral. It'd been a day full of rage, thunderstorms, and tears.

People didn't understand the reasoning behind his anger at God, and it was a secret that Ethan and his sister tried to withhold between the two of them.

When Ethan was the age of five, and his sister, eight, their real father still roamed the earth. Prowling like a lion hunts his prey.

Ethan shuddered at the distant memories that still seemed too close for comfort.

Peter Wallace. An alcoholic. A drug addict. A cruel person. Looking back at it, Ethan wasn't sure if he could even call Peter "Dad." The images of Peter abusing Ethan's mother were forever imbedded in his memory. His mom was always too afraid to speak her mind and stand up for herself. It didn't make her a wimp, she had been a strong woman in the end.

Peter raised his voice at Sara and Ethan more than Ethan would ever be able to number. He even physically abused the two of them when his anger intensified. Ethan feared life when he woke up in the morning as a kid. Sara would wail every time Peter would come close to her. At age five and eight, the most they should have had to worry about was which Lego went where.

Ethan touched his forearm, rubbing his fingers over a scar his real father had created from snatching Ethan by the arm. He could still smell the blood. Hear his mother wailing in the bathroom. All these memories caused his body to tremor as he put his truck into Park in front of the community church Mark pastored.

When he turned seven, Ethan's first grade teacher curiously asked about his black eye, and he spilled his guts to her about his abusive father. Being an honest kid, he didn't miss a single detail whilst telling her. Later that evening when Ethan and Sara trudged off the school bus, cops and ambulances surrounded his house, but no one seemed to be in a hurry. He didn't spy anyone arresting Peter. Instead, they were carrying his birth father out in a body bag. Peter had shot and killed himself when he heard sirens in the driveway. Only eight, Ethan didn't understand all the mass confusion going on around him.

A cop had met Ethan and Sara in the driveway as the school bus drove away. Nathaniel Grey. The heroic cop that Ethan would never forget. The man who later became the father Ethan had never received.

Nathan explained what was going on around them, and Ethan just buried his head in the cop's arms. He desired for someone to care about him, and the affectionate cop did just that. Nathaniel spent days checking on Ethan and Sara's mom, Kate, and him and his sister. As a kid growing up in the situation he did, it took forever for Ethan to trust in someone again. Trust was an issue. Not for Sara though. She loved the father figure at first sight.

After months of taking Ethan and Sara out for ice cream, fishing, hunting, and teaching Ethan how to flirt, Nathaniel became an important person to Ethan. Not only to Ethan and Sara, but to their mom as well. Kate had fallen in love with the devoted Christian man Nathan was.

Ethan was nine when Nathaniel came to him and Sara and asked permission to marry their mom. In that moment, nothing seemed more exciting than welcoming a real father into their family. Nathaniel was a father that centered God, church events, and the Bible in the midst of their family. He provided a hope for them. Their entire family accepted Jesus Christ into their hearts. Family had more of a meaning to it in that merciful second chance. Blood relations didn't hold as much as an importance. It was

God, unity, joy, and so much love that made their family stick like glue.

Nathaniel had been a blessing, and so had his mom...for God to take that blessing away from Ethan, it upset him. It turned his world upside down. For six months after Kate and Nathan had been in the car crash, he wrestled around the question of why God would do that to him and his sister. Although they were old enough to live on their own, they were still left alone. He decided then that it was easier to believe there was no God, than to wrap his head around the *why's*, *how's*, and raging anger.

That resulted in the was the person Ethan was today. The longer he dwelled on his past though, the more concerned he became. Bile rose in his throat as he suddenly realized he was morphing into his birth father. His hands quaked at the thought. No matter if there was a God or not, he couldn't accept the fact that he was sending his sister back through that pain again. They wouldn't have each other this time...Sara only had herself. Ethan had to stop drinking and grow up. He just had to.

Mark had taken a day off duty just to meet him. That proved to Ethan where Mark's priorities were. He'd never met a police officer so devoted to something else in his life other than his job, especially having the role of police chief in Alton. He could already tell that the man was driven by his passion of faith and beliefs.

His sister was right. He needed this. He needed to recover.

"You don't look hungover this morning." Hope quirked an eyebrow as she poured his cup of coffee and sat it down on the counter.

"I had only two bottles last night," Ethan stated with a smile.

Hope didn't know the regular amount that he consumed, so she assumed that two bottles were better than his usual number. The fact that he was trying said something. He wanted to take a different path. Hope just prayed that this new path led him to Jesus.

Ethan had started coming back to the café yesterday morning, ordering mixed berry streusel muffins instead. She didn't know why, but Hope was elated to see him walk through the door. There was something about him that made her heart go full speed like her electric mixer.

"Progress is good." Hope smiled. She took an older woman's order and poured her a coffee to go, along with a bag of cream cheese Danishes. Once she finished, she sat back down on the barstool across from him and sighed. "It's been a busy morning."

"How did interviews go last week?" Ethan took a sip of coffee, trying to make small talk with her as she took orders every now and then.

She snarled her nose. "Long, but successful. We hired two more people to help behind the counter, and three in the kitchen. I definitely appreciate the extra hands now, we work efficiently for the most part. We're all adapting to each other and I'm enjoying having them around."

He nodded. "Your schedule has settled down a bit then, hasn't it?"

"Depends on what you're trying to get at." Hope glanced down at her hands folded over each other on the countertop, trying to stop the blush that unwillingly crept to her cheeks.

Ethan chuckled. "Would you like to join my sister and I for dinner Saturday evening? Sara would love your company."

She smiled at the way he worded it. "Oh, so you wouldn't love the company?"

"It's an excuse to make you feel guilty. That way you have to come."

"I see." She smirked. "Can you cook?"

He laughed before he even answered, a sure sign that he could not. "I can try to. If Chinese takeout is on the counter instead, don't judge."

She snickered at his statement. "I'll look forward to it."

"Maybe I can get Sara to cook." He quirked an eyebrow and added a mischievous grin, after a moment of silence.

"Yeah, she'll get right on that." Hope laughed. "The poor girl could barely carry a pot without wincing right now."

He shrugged his shoulders. "I could try." The smirk on Ethan's face told Hope all she needed to know.

"She'll tell you no." Hope had only known Sara for a week now, but she already knew what kind of relationship Sara and Ethan had. It was an amusing one full of jokes, bluntness, and teasing.

"Then be prepared for takeout." He grimaced.

"You can cook. For some reason, I have some sort of faith in you. Besides, if it's a grilled cheese I'll be happy." She winked and went around refilling coffee cups. She stopped for a moment back at Ethan's seat. "If you cook, I'll bring ingredients to make a dessert," Hope added, sending a convincing look his way. She even wiggled her eyebrows.

It was like watching a puppy's ear perk up at the sound of the word *treat*. His grin was incredible. "You've got yourself a deal."

"Do you have something you would prefer to learn to make...or just eat?" Hope laughed as she pointed toward the display counter.

"The éclairs for sure. They're my second favorite." He grinned and played with his empty coffee cup.

"Excellent choice."

Ethan stood up, stretched, and grabbed his leather jacket. "If you'll excuse me, I've got counseling to go to." He left her a tip, which she thanked him for.

"Don't let my brother be too hard on you. If he is, send me and I'll fix it." Hope grinned, knowing that Mark would never be too rude or too hard on a person like Ethan, or any person really. It was fun to tease though.

"He's a good guy with good intentions." He smiled. "Plus, he's like you. A softie." He headed toward the door.

Hope tilted her head to the side. "I don't know whether that's a good thing, or a terrible thing."

"Believe me, it's a good thing." He winked and walked out the door that jingled behind him.

Hope felt heat rise to her neck first, then to her ears, and finally, her cheeks. She smiled as she watched Ethan walk away on the sidewalk. There was something about him, but she couldn't place her finger on it. He seemed different. Hope shook herself out of her daze and made her way back to the kitchen.

seven

"**B**estest is not a word, Mark." Bri chewed on the end of her pen as she stared her brother down.

"It is in my dictionary," he retorted, throwing a piece of popcorn her way. He missed her, and his golden retriever puppy scampered its way over to eat it.

"I'm not counting it."

"Add the points to my score," he begged.

"No."

"You're just mad because I wouldn't count your insane, made up word." Mark stuck his tongue out at her.

"It was a *Z* on a triple point space!"

"It wasn't even pronounceable, Bri." Hope's brother narrowed his eyebrows at their youngest sister.

Hope shook her head, snorting at the bickering her siblings were in the middle of. Scrabble was a game that Mark and Brianna never failed to make an intense competition.

They were gathered at Mark's cute, cabin-like home on a calm Thursday evening to watch the Chicago Bears play. Hope was cozied up on Mark's shaggy rug, dressed in her sweats, with a slice of a local Italian diner's pizza in her hand. It didn't get much better than this. She enjoyed evenings with her brother and sister, it was always entertaining.

"Hope, it's your turn," Mark grumbled. He'd removed the word *BESTEST* off the board and replaced it with *THE*.

"Very original." Hope cackled at his word.

"You two are just jealous. I didn't choose the simple life; the simple life chose me." He tossed another piece of popcorn in the dog's direction.

"You're making Snoopy gain weight." Hope referred to Mark's dog that was begging for more human food. Mark loved Charlie Brown films, so that was where the puppy gained its name. Mark had rescued him from a shelter. The owners didn't want Snoopy, so Mark expanded the family a bit. He had a soft spot for animals, but he would never admit it.

"A little chubby never killed nobody." He shrugged. "This dog is a growin' pup." The puppy brought Mark a slightly chewed tennis ball and Mark tossed it across the living room for the dog to fetch.

Bri chuckled as Snoopy dove for the ball and face planted into a wall. "I'm going to grab a soda. Anyone want one?"

"I'll take a Cola." Mark took up his sister's offer, then laughed at Snoopy as he pranced back with the ball in his mouth.

"Make that two." Hope batted her eyelashes as she watched Brianna make her way to Mark's kitchen.

"I wonder if she will consider being my maid and do everything for me?" Mark grinned. Their younger sister did anything and *every*thing at their request. When they were kids, they gave Bri the role of supplying their very needs when they were too lazy to fulfill them themselves. Like Bri always being the one to bring them all back peanut butter and jelly sandwiches when they were playing in the tree house in their backyard. Now they just plain teased her about it.

"She has to do it with the title *sister*. She won't hold the title of being a maid." Hope chuckled and played the word *QUIXOTRY* on a *Q* already placed on the board. Mark snarled at the word that, with perfect placement, earned her three hundred and sixty-five points.

Hope hopped up from the floor and settled into Mark's comfy leather couch, satisfied with her turn. They'd been sitting on the floor, hunched over the coffee table, trying to finish their Scrabble game that was taking over an hour. She was getting sick of coming up with words to put on the board and her back was getting stiff, but the company of her siblings made it worthwhile.

"How's counseling with Ethan going?" Hope asked, hoping her brother wouldn't mind the question. Mark normally didn't talk about other's problems when he worked with people who had addictions, but this time it was important to Hope. She needed to at least know if it was going somewhat well from someone other than Ethan's point of view.

"He's opened up a little bit more over the past two weeks. We've talked about why he started drinking. I've given him a couple Bible verses to look at, but I don't want to pressure or guilt him into anything." He took a seat beside her on the couch.

"Has he mentioned anything else to you?" Hope picked at one of her chipped nails that had broken. She *desperately* needed a manicure.

"Other than his parents? No. We've went through everything that's happened from the car crash, up until now. Why do you ask?"

"I think we're missing something. There's a bigger picture that he's not telling us about. He never goes into detail about his past, before he lost his parents. Where are all his happy memories?"

Mark considered it. "You're most likely on to something, I'll write a reminder in my journal." He rested his head back on the black leather couch.

"He asked me to dinner with his sister and him, Saturday evening." Hope bit her lip, hoping her brother wouldn't look too far into the friendly offer Ethan made earlier in the day.

"I know." His comment threw Hope off.

She sat straight up. "How?"

"He asked me if it'd be okay before he asked you." Mark met her eyes while a slight smirk played on his lips.

Hope couldn't help but blush. It was sweet that Ethan took that much consideration into his gestures. "He's just a friend."

"He's nice, and not half bad of a guy, but take some advice from a guy who has seen a lot. Don't lead him on…not until he's stable." He paused, taking time to carefully choose his words. "He needs God, Hope. And you need a Godly man."

Hope absorbed every ounce of what Mark advised her to do. She needed a firm in his faith kind of man to lead her. She had to pray for him, even if she didn't know who he would be yet. She had to pray that he would be exactly what she needed, not what she wanted, for necessities were far more important than wants.

Hope also had to look at the other side of her prayer too. Her future husband would need a Godly woman to support his calling and passions. Someone that would stand on God's truth and never veer the wrong way. She needed to examine more of herself before she thought more about want she needed in a partner for life. Hope decided then to start sincerely looking more into who God needed her to be.

Ethan needed God to change his life—the direction of it, and the perspective of it. Then, Hope might consider him more than a friend. Until then, she needed to wait it out. God had a plan, and she trusted Him.

"Thank you." Hope smiled at her older brother. She simply didn't know what she'd do without her older brother. God had placed Mark in her life for a reason, even if it was just to run over her toes with his battery-operated Mustang.

It was more than that, but she laughed silently at her thoughts.

"Something smells delicious." Hope followed Ethan through his house.

His house was a rather large, two-story modern farmhouse. Hope immediately felt at home with the white wood accents and the floor to ceiling windows allowing room for plenty of natural light. She would be lying if she said she didn't love it.

The exquisite home sat upon acres on acres of open land that was placed on the top of a hill. The sunset view would be incredible. She didn't know Ethan's plans for the evening, but she'd have to ask for time to watch the sunset. She found there wasn't a sunset God painted that she didn't like.

"I'm sorry I couldn't pick you up. I would have, but Sara made me cook after all. She and I both want your lovely dessert." He grinned and shoved his hands in his pockets. Ethan was dressed in a pair of dark blue jeans and a black long sleeve shirt that traced his biceps. Hope was relieved when she saw his casual look, for she picked a simple, oversized navy sweater and faded black jeggings.

"It was no problem. I'm hungry, so I'm glad it worked out." She caused him to chuckle.

"Sara's in the kitchen. She's overworking herself. Please make her sit down. She won't listen to a single thing I say."

"If I didn't know any better I would have thought you were talking about a child." She laughed as he led her into the kitchen.

Ethan pulled the sliding barn door that separated the kitchen from the spacious living room. Hope's eyes bulged at the baker's heaven that she just stepped into.

The kitchen was beautiful in it's all white glory. A large marbled island sat in the center with shiplap cascading down the sides. Hope couldn't wait to use it while she made dessert. The kitchen in her apartment was far too compact for her liking, she'd enjoy borrowing Ethan's for an evening. Although bright white, the cupboards had a wooden, rustic farmhouse look to them, which made the kitchen cozy. She was already envisioning her pastel kitchen utensils atop the white marbled countertops. They would add such a cute pop of color.

"Your home is gorgeous," she gushed.

Ethan chuckled at her reaction. "Thank you. It was my mom and dad's." He seemed proud of it. And he also didn't look upset at his own mention of his parents. Hope smiled as she denoted the slow progress. The fact that he still lived in the same home after losing his parents told Hope that Ethan had roots bound here that couldn't just be left unattended to. She admired him for that. He was stronger than he thought.

"I'm going out to clean up the table under the pergola. I hope you don't mind, it shouldn't be too cold to eat outside this evening." He headed toward the back door and Hope grinned. It meant she'd get to see the sunset. "Make yourself at home. Sara should be in here somewhere. I figure you'll enjoy the kitchen."

"Already have." She smiled as he walked outside through the sliding glass door in the kitchen.

She set her bag of supplies to make the éclairs on the kitchen island. This place was too neat and gorgeous for a drunk to be living in it. It made her wonder why he put himself in the position he was in. Obviously, it was more complex than the simple thought she was pondering on, but the question still lingered in the back of her mind.

She wandered around the kitchen for any sight of Sara.

A tart burner in the corner of a counter filled the room with a cupcake-like scent. It had to be a touch Sara added. She couldn't see Ethan being the type to burn tarts. She snickered at that.

"Sara?" Hope called.

After a few moments she received a response. "In here."

She followed a voice that led to what looked like a cabinet in the opposite corner of the tart burner. Hope moved beside of the massive refrigerator and listened for movement. She pulled the tall cabinet door open and had to keep her jaw from touching the whitewashed hardwood floor. It wasn't just a tall cabinet; it was a walk-in pantry! The gigantic pantry was full of shelves holding all sorts of labeled jars, baking supplies, spices, and non-perishable foods. Ethan and Sara's parents had to have been wealthy. The entire place was absolutely jaw dropping, and Ethan had inherited what looked like all of it.

Hope found Sara rummaging in the corner for something on a shelf. "Do you see garlic anywhere?" Sara frowned.

"I did not picture Ethan being this organized." Still in awe, Hope searched for a jar labeled *Garlic*.

"He may not cook often, but he's oddly particular about what he does have," Sara said.

Hope took a mental note of what Sara informed her on.

"Ah, here it is." Sara grabbed a jar stuffed with garlic flakes and headed out of the pantry and toward the oven. She sat the jar down on the island. "Now, shall we say a proper hello?" She giggled and gave Hope a welcoming, warm hug.

"How are you doing, Sara?" Hope smiled and hopped onto one of the barstools at the island.

"Pain comes and goes but lifting a five-pound weight isn't as bad anymore." Sara chuckled. "It's all about progress, so it's going well."

"You look great." Hope beamed. "And might I add that whatever you've helped Ethan cook up smells great." Hope nodded toward the oven.

"We won't tell him that I've been supervising when he steps out of the kitchen," she whispered and then let out a laugh. "He made most of it, but he had to ask me how to cook it about a million times. Then he wrote it down, but I kept an eye on it. He tends to burn things." The girls giggled.

Sara pulled out what looked like a pan of French bread from the oven, sprinkled some garlic and cheese on top, and then set the pan back in the oven to broil. "I hope you like Italian. Baked spaghetti is on the menu."

"It's one of my favorites." Hope smiled. "Could I stick the filling for the éclairs in the fridge?"

"Of course. It's a fridge big enough for two or three humans to fit in. There's room."

Hope laughed. "Remind me not to make you angry, you might stuff me in Ethan's fridge."

"You're already too good a friend." Sara snickered and grabbed the baked spaghetti from the oven.

Hope opened the refrigerator doors and didn't have to search hard for a place to put her baking goodies. She froze when she saw two brand new cases of beer in Ethan's fridge, along with many half empty whiskey bottles. Tears threatened to spill down Hope's eyes. The realization that Ethan planned on drinking even more hurt her heart.

He was a drunk, what did she expect? It broke her though, to see it firsthand. To hear about it was one thing, but to physically see it made a difference. It was an addiction that gradually beat the man mentally, physically, and spiritually, until he died. Alcohol was a murderer. Ethan had the desire to stop, Hope could see it in his despairing eyes. Yet, his taste buds and mind were tricking him into thinking he needed more and more.

Sara must have noticed Hope's movement abruptly come to a halt, for she was by Hope's side within seconds. She realized what Hope was staring at and placed a hand on Hope's shoulder. "Relax, Hope. He really is making progress. I've seen it. We just have to accept that the process might be slower than what we want or expect. Plus, he won't magically get better. He needs Jesus to make that happen."

Hope nodded. "It's hard to imagine the battle raging in his mind; wanting to do better, but everything in him is telling him he can't."

"He has a sister who can pray for him now, and I'm not giving up. Between counseling with Mark, your sister, you, and me, I believe we can get Ethan back to the person he once used to be." Sara spoke with so much positivity. Her renewed faith with God glistened and it inspired Hope. "I plan on being at church tomorrow morning. I'm feeling well enough to sit through a service without my neck screaming at me," she added with a gleaming smile.

"I'll be sure to save you a seat." Hope smiled, then began to help Sara prepare the dishes to bring out on the patio. All the while, she prayed that the war in Ethan's heart would settle. That he would discover a hope that was everlasting.

After a yummy dinner, baking, eating too many éclairs to count, followed by a comedy movie Ethan had picked out, a long walk was much needed. Sara called it a night after the éclairs and went to bed upstairs in Ethan's home. According to Ethan, Sara's house was just over the hill, but she was staying with him until she fully recovered. The house that Sara claimed as her own was once Ethan and Sara's grandparents' house. It looked like a cozy cabin that Hope would love to pay a visit to sometime.

Ethan suggested he and Hope go on a walk around his private and peaceful property, and Hope was immensely enjoying it. The wind blowing through the fields and the trickle of a stream near the woods were both something she could get used to, for she never enjoyed large, crowded places. She could see herself reading a book by the small pond in the field and not giving a care to the rest of the world around her.

The night was coming to an end, and strangely, Hope didn't want it to. It felt good to hang out with new friends. She enjoyed the company. Resting on a wooden bench, she watched Ethan skip rocks over the bright filtered pond with fish swimming in it. The colorful setting sun made the night peaceful. It was a wonderful way to end a pleasurable night.

"Thank you for this evening. I'm glad to know Sara's back on her own two feet." Hope watched as Ethan made his way to sit beside her.

"Come over more often. I've had a wonderful time." The corners of Ethan's mouth crinkled, gratitude spreading across his face. "Thank you for it."

"Oh, I'll be back. Even if it is just to sit by the pond and feed the ducks." Hope chuckled.

"They're already getting fat. Sara's been feeding them cheese puffs." He snorted. Ethan's eyes wandered over to Hope's. She could see an awaiting topic of discussion in his kiwi frosting colored eyes. "Your brother gave me a Bible verse this week."

Hope's heart was glad she didn't have to bring the topic up herself; this time Ethan was stretching it forward himself. She licked her lips. "Which one?"

"First Corinthians chapter fifteen and verse fifty-five, *'O death, where is thy sting? O grave, where is thy victory?'*" He stopped there, and Hope understood why. Ethan couldn't grasp the fact that if he or others believed and trusted in God, there would be no loss in death, the grave wouldn't hold them back.

She tried to be careful choosing her words. "God never intended for man to die, Ethan. And He certainly doesn't bring

115

terrible things to happen in your life, not without a cause to make something beautiful from it, of course. God tempts not one person. Does that mean that awful things won't occur in your life? Absolutely not, because you live in this nutty world. Bad things are going to come across this crazy path we call life, but that doesn't mean that we should shun God." She caught his gaze; his face was solemn. "God is so magnificently powerful that He can take the bad things in life and work them for good and for His glory. Whatever you do, please don't accuse God for what happened to your parents.

"Read the book of Job. Job lost *every*thing, but the very first thing he did was praise God." She inhaled a deep breath. *Thank you for those words, God. You speak in a still small voice, yet You are so powerful. Touch Ethan's broken heart.*

Hope watched as he ran his fingers through his curly hair. Ethan needed peace. He needed to trust God. He was twenty-five and already looked three or four years older than his actual age. He needed hope before this addiction completely ate him up. It was swallowing his past and making it ten times worse than it had to be.

116

"Do you really believe in Heaven…that there's an afterlife full of harmony and joy?"

"I do." Her answer was simple and firm. She wasn't going to compromise it, not even for an incredibly handsome guy sitting beside her.

"I don't think I can." His head hung low as he shut his eyes at the words Hope knew he didn't believe. He was battling it out with himself, and if he was not careful, he'd let himself win and give into giving up.

It'd be easier for him to believe in Heaven and take comfort knowing his parents were there, than to place the blame directly on his shoulders. Ethan made the pressure intense when he didn't need to. If he just gave it to God instead… "Christ defeated death when He arose, that gives hope beyond the grave, Ethan. Seeing how you said your parents believed and trusted in God, it's a peaceful reassurance to trust in." The breeze blew Hope's straight hair around her face. She was getting cold, it was getting late, and she needed to go home. "Sara is coming to church in the morning. Would you like to join us?"

Ethan immediately shook his head "Maybe another time." He straightened himself and stood from the bench. He grabbed Hope's hand to help her up.

Hope only nodded, for she didn't want to guilt him.

There was a long string of semi-comfortable silence between the two of them as they walked to Hope's vehicle. "Thank you for dinner and thank you for letting me get to know you a bit better. Don't eat all the leftover éclairs at once." Hope snickered. She wanted to leave the night on a light, happy note.

"We will do something again soon, even if it is just you and me. Sara took almost all the leftovers to her room. You should feel sorry for me." He made a puppy face that could have defeated an actual puppy.

"Woe is Ethan." She mocked as she hopped into her car and rolled down the window. She was glad he was suggesting another day for them soon. They'd be good friends, she decided.

"Woe is me." He chuckled, shoving his hands in his pockets and kicking up loose gravel as he watched her drive away.

eight

"Mom, that looks stunning." Hope placed her hands on her hips and stared at the Christmas tree in awe. The tree that Hope and Brianna picked out was artificial, full, tall, and white with colorful twinkling lights. For the finishing touch, her mom hung pastel pink glittered cooking utensil ornaments on the limbs. It was like looking at a Barbie doll Christmas tree, very girly.

Hope smiled as she watched her mom, Heather, decorate the Christmas tree in the corner of the bakery. It was a Lawson tradition to always decorate the tree weeks before Thanksgiving. The tradition was being kept this year. Hope was thrilled to have her parents back in the United States from a recent mission trip to Uganda. Just the thought of being all together for the upcoming Holidays made Hope's heart feel warm and fuzzy.

"When I saw these ornaments, I immediately thought of you and Bri." Hope's mom beamed as she took a step back to approve of the tree. "The lady back in Uganda was making these to use the money to feed her family. So, I made for sure to buy plenty." Heather winked at Hope.

Gratitude filled Hope's heart. The wisdom filled woman had become her best friend. Heather had long, silky chocolate hair the same color as Mark's, although it was growing more silver as she aged gracefully. She wore a new wooly scarf a kid in Uganda helped her make. Her mom owned more scarves than Hope would ever be able to count.

Hope's mom always supported her and her siblings for as long as she could remember. She loved them enough to teach them to pursue the dreams God designed for them to fulfil. Heather was the reason behind Hope's passion for making desserts. She taught Hope how to make Oreo balls when she was thirteen and Hope fell in love with concocting new recipes. Brianna always played the role of Hope's trustee sidekick, whilst Mark and her dad, Steven, snuck in to lick the beaters or taste test.

"I love them! Thank you." Hope handed a steaming cup full of chamomile tea to her mom. "I'm making Dad's favorite pumpkin spice cupcakes for Thanksgiving on Thursday." Her dad would protest if Hope made anything else, for the pumpkin cupcakes were his favorite.

"He'll love that." Her mom took a seat at the counter as Hope boxed up blueberry muffin cookies for a pick-up order later this evening. "Will you be joining Bri and I for some crazy Black Friday shopping?" She raised her eyebrows.

"Wouldn't miss it for the world. I love getting to see my mom in full shopping mode. I might have to bring a video camera this time." They both laughed at Hope's comment. Visions of her mom running down the aisles of Target were forever embedded in her family's, and probably all Target employees', memory.

"Would you mind if I brought a friend?" Hope planned on bringing Ethan's sister, Sara. They bonded quite a bit over the past couple weeks. She figured Sara could use some extra girl time.

"The more the merrier." Her mom smiled. "Steven and Mark have already opted out. Mark's surprising your dad with tickets to a Chicago Bears game." Heather's green eyes beamed.

Hope stopped what she was doing and waited for her mom inform her it was a joke. But she never did. "You're kidding," Hope replied.

"Nope. He has a plan on how to surprise him and everything. They're making an extra-long weekend of it." She took a sip of her tea and grinned.

"And to think, I supply him with cupcakes." Hope scoffed. "I better be next." She laughed.

It was worse tonight. *Much worse.*

"Start with something simple. Like when your lips crave a drink, grab an Oreo cookie instead." Mark's words from their most recent therapy session rang in Ethan's ears.

Oreo cookies were his favorite, but he had already gone through two family size packages in the past two days. He was going to get fat on cream filled cookies. This wasn't working.

Gripping the sink counter, Ethan pulled himself up from the cold bathroom floor. He stared at the four by six picture he'd been clutching onto. It was of him with his parents at his high school graduation. He'd found it in the back of his closet earlier and it'd sparked tonight's explosion. Standing on the soccer field, his mother, freckles in full bloom, kissed Ethan on his cheek while his stepdad beamed proudly at Ethan's side.

A million memories hit him like a crashing wave. His senior year had been one of his favorites. If Ethan closed his eyes, he

124

could hear his parents cheering Ethan on as he played on the soccer field. He could smell his mother's sweet perfume as she ran from the stands to engulf him in a hug. He could feel his true father pat him on the back. The memories were too strong.

He'd lost it all. His family. His friends. His dignity. It was all gone.

Heaving out deep breaths, he stared at his reflection in the mirror. His face was red and blotchy, and his eyes were bloodshot. A person observing him would have thought he was a drug addict by the way he was shaking. *One step forward, two steps back.*

Ethan thought he was improving, but tonight had been a major setback. The holidays coming up that used to be full of excitement, were now dreadful. He didn't want to accept the fact that his parents wouldn't be here for another Thanksgiving. His mom wouldn't be cooking his favorite homemade brown gravy and singing Christmas carols as she did so. His stepdad wouldn't be putting up the tree and helping carve the turkey. It wasn't the same—it would never be the same…and it broke Ethan's heart.

He staggered, journeying toward the kitchen. On his way, he seemed to have knocked something over because shards of glass shattered behind him. Instead of turning around to see what he had broken, he continued on his mission for the sensation that his tongue ached for. When his foot began to burn, Ethan glanced down. Blurs marred his vision, but he could clearly see the blood. He could smell the coppery odor. The glass had cut him.

Ethan almost stopped to observe how bad the cut was, but *no*. That didn't matter right now. He fixated his eyes on the fridge as he hobbled into the kitchen. Swinging the refrigerator door open, he opted for a whiskey bottle instead of another beer.

After two shots of whiskey, he poured the rest of the bottle down the drain. Ethan gripped the sides of the sink to steady himself. Once the first tear fell from his eye, the rest broke lose like a dam that had finally burst wide open as he dwelled on his wretched condition. His breath shuttered as he tried to inhale deeply.

He needed his sister here tonight. He needed her to tell him he should have chocolate milk instead. Alcohol used to dissolve all of Ethan's problems and stress. It used to bring euphoria, but recently it had been throwing his past at him and gnawing at him more than he could handle. Ethan felt like a cord being chomped on by a rat.

Nathaniel had been the God-sent hope Ethan needed after Peter killed himself. Nathaniel had been Ethan's way of letting go of his past and putting hope and trust in the future…in God.

Who's going to help me get out of this black hole that I'm in now? The question rocked his mind as he began to feel dizzy.

He swallowed the lump in his throat. Making his way to the corner of the counter, he tried his very best to focus on where his phone was. After several attempts, he finally grasped it in his hand. He dialed Hope's phone number, making for sure to punch in the right numbers. He only called her a handful of times before now. He would've called his sister, but he vaguely remembered Sara being in pain after her long day of physical therapy. He needed Hope.

Hope's cell phone incessantly rang like an annoying crow at the crack of dawn.

She rolled over in her bed and groaned. It had already been a long day at the bakery. People were filing in left and right for last minute Thanksgiving desserts.

She glanced at her alarm clock before answering her phone. *3:02 A.M.*

Who would be calling this early in the morning?

Her heart rate sped up at the possible thought that someone in her family could be hurt, or worse…her brother could have run into trouble with his job.

She answered the phone, not taking time to look at the number. "Hello?"

"Hope, I *need* you." Hope's heart immediately sank as she recognized the slurred voice.

Ethan.

He fumbled with his words. If he was as depressed as he sounded, it was hard to tell what was running through his mind tonight.

"I'll be over in ten minutes. In the meantime, grab a sports drink. The electrolytes will help," Hope replied, not even bothering to ask what was wrong. Worry filled her mind.

God, please don't let Ethan do anything foolish tonight.

"Be careful on the roads." He slowly gathered his thoughts. "It's starting to snow." Even if he was drunk, Hope could still hear in his desperate voice that he cared.

She stood up and stretched, then glanced out the curtains by her bay window. It indeed was snowing. "Always."

She hung up the phone and pulled an old high school sweatshirt on, along with a pair of jeans. Hope laced up a pair of sneakers and shoved her phone in her back pocket in case of an emergency. She quickly strode to her bathroom barely big enough to move around in, to brush her teeth and pull her hair back into a sloppy looking bun.

She brewed a cup of coffee to go and dumped a bunch of creamer and sugar in it. It was going to be cold, and she needed to stay awake as she drove. She'd have another cup once she got to Ethan's place, even if the taste wasn't pleasant to her taste buds. Early mornings were not her thing. She was a bear most mornings, but this morning she would try her best to be an angel.

"I can't believe your mom let you dye your hair red." Hope's laughter echoed through Ethan's house.

Their friendship had been taken to another level tonight. She arrived hours earlier to an Ethan that she'd never seen before. His door was unlocked, and she found him curled in the corner of his kitchen with a bloody foot. Nothing had prepared her for tonight's scene. It was only by the grace of God that she'd put herself to work by bandaging his wounded foot and cleaning up shards of glass instead of panicking.

Alcohol depressed Ethan more than he did to himself when he was sober. Hope gingerly tried to calm him as she helped him gain a clear head.

It had been hard to get him to speak with her at first, but after she'd placed a hand on his quivering shoulder and told him she was there for him, he'd spent minutes crying on her shoulder. Never had she met a man more broken than Ethan. He was at war with himself. Wanting to do right, but not able to give alcohol up.

She never wanted to see another episode as she did tonight. Ethan was capable of so much more. She just knew it.

Hope tucked a loose hair behind her ear as she flipped through Ethan's family photo albums. She suggested he look at something happy tonight, for he needed some happiness in his life. It had been tough at first but being there with him made it easier. Good memories helped. Ethan finally settled into the grey couch beside of her and was half-laughing. It felt good to see a smile on his face. He was a lot more attractive that way.

"I wanted to be a clown for Halloween and I wasn't going to take an itchy wig all day. So, Mom gave me some cash and sent me to the store. I didn't know I bought

131

permanent hair dye." Hope watched as Ethan cringed at the memory. "I think I still have the red towel that used to be white around here somewhere." He chuckled as she flipped through the album.

"Oh, my goodness, look at this!" Hope pointed to a picture of Ethan dressed as Elvis Presley with his hair slicked back. He wore thick rim glasses, a white bedazzled suit, and a guitar by his side. "You were so cute." Hope laughed.

"*Were*? Am I not now?" Ethan fished for compliments.

"I didn't mean it that way," Hope replied, keeping her eyes glued on the album.

"So, you think I'm still cute?" A smirk formed across his face.

She felt her cheeks get hot. She wasn't going to admit that he was not *just* cute. He was handsome. She would keep that comment to herself, though. "You're not bad." She wrinkled her nose as she looked up at him, teasing him.

He elbowed her in the side. "You're not bad either *and* you have a heart of gold.

Not many girls have that now a day." Ethan rested his back into the faux leather couch.

Hope knew her cheeks were bound to be a deep crimson color by now.

"You're blushing." Ethan grinned and laid his head back on a plaid pillow.

Hope could feel his eyes on her as she paged through the photo book full of memories. "And *you're* tired," she remarked.

Ethan only laughed.

Hope stopped flipping through the photo album when she came across a picture of Ethan's mom. "Your mom was beautiful." His mother's face was naturally beautiful. Freckles all over, long eyelashes that made her emerald eyes pop, and a dimpled smile just like Ethan's. Her gorgeous wavy chestnut hair was framed around her face ever so elegantly. Sara favored their mom.

"I agree." The pained look on his face told Hope that his mom held a special place in his heart.

Hope flipped to the next page. "Who's this?" She stopped at a picture of Ethan smiling with his mom on what looked

133

like his birthday. Hope pointed to a man, on the left of them, holding a beer can in one hand and a cigarette in the other. He looked as if he were in a daze. And from his grubby dress, he seemed as if he didn't care the least bit about his appearance.

"I thought you said your dad was a Christian?" She frowned as she compared the picture in the album to a picture frame set out on Ethan's side table by the couch.

It wasn't the same man.

She glanced from the pictures to Ethan, who hadn't been responding to her questions. His frozen stature told Hope that she had come across something she wasn't supposed to discover. Her heart cracked as she saw his jaw lock and a tear fall down his cheek. Hope knew right then that she discovered the root to all his problems. This was the *something* she knew he had been holding out on her.

He could have lied to her, but for some reason he found it easier to tell the truth. Ethan hadn't been thinking when he let Hope flip through the old photo albums. His birth father never crossed his mind. Ethan hadn't thought he owned pictures of Peter anymore…obviously, he'd been wrong.

Ethan spilled everything to Hope. From being abused by his real father, Peter committing suicide, how his mom and Nathaniel met—everything up until now. Hope just sat there, soaking up even the microscopic details like a sponge. She didn't say much of anything as Ethan explained his whole life history. To his dismay, she didn't seem hurt by the fact that Ethan hadn't told her the full story from the beginning. Instead, she seemed hurt for him.

It felt strange for someone other than his sister to know about the life he had before his stepfather came along…for someone to perceive the entire truth behind his life and the way he lived it. He'd kept Peter a secret for so long because he'd hoped it would all go away, but it never had. More than that though, it felt like an enclosed barrel had been removed from around his body. The walls he'd held up for so long had come crashing down. It finally felt like the air wasn't as thick anymore. Maybe this was what he'd needed.

They had moved from the living room to the kitchen, for Hope insisted that coffee would be a promising idea. Although, Ethan would have rather ran for the hills. He sat across the table from her, wishing he could give her the world...but he couldn't even give himself a clear conscious.

"Ethan." Hope took his hand in hers and she gave it a gentle squeeze. The warmth of her fingers went straight to Ethan's core. "You do understand that drinking isn't helping this matter and it never will, right?" Her intriguing green eyes met his.

"I know." He rested his elbows on the kitchen table and placed his head between his hands. The realization had been there from the moment he had taken the first sip of alcohol. It was a mistake from the beginning, yet the alcohol consumed him more and more, and Ethan simply welcomed it right into his life's door.

Hope sipped on what Ethan believed was her fourth cup of mainly creamer, with a little dash of coffee. "Your birth father made bad decisions Ethan, but that doesn't mean that you have to follow in his footsteps. Think of Nathaniel—the loving stepdad—all the joy he had. You said yourself he didn't have a sip of alcohol. He also had God by his side. Look back at how happy your family was then. Don't you realize that God was the reason behind it?"

Ethan made no comment. His heart felt like his cold, empty coffee mug. He knew the truth, but he was frozen in his own selfishness.

"God is faithful and just. When we put our trust in Him, He stills our hearts and thoughts. Because He has been faithful throughout history, we can trust Him in times of trouble. That's what your family did after Peter. You guys trusted in God. Why not trust Him again for this battle?"

That was the thing, he wasn't ready to trust again. What if God let him down again? It wasn't a commitment Ethan was willing to make when he didn't know of the unknown. "He's let me down so many times. If God were real, wouldn't you think there'd be some extent of mercy? Why does it feel like He abandoned me?" It felt like a pitiful excuse, but his questions were sincere.

"I don't mean to sound cold Ethan, but God didn't walk out on you. *You* walked

137

out on *Him*." The truth slapped him in the face, but Hope kept a sympathetic smile on her face, showing that she wasn't meaning to hurt him. "As hard as it is to swallow that tough pill, we have to accept that sometimes terrible things will happen in life. But God can mold the bad into good. That's what He did when He sent your family Nathaniel. Don't you want believe in some sort of hope this time?"

"I'm hopeless," he replied as he sulked back into his chair.

Hope straightened her back and crooked her neck. Her eyes seemed to flicker an emotion. Maybe concern? "Why do you think that?"

"I've lost *all* of my parents, my dignity, my reputation. A few family members in other states don't want to have anything to do with me anymore. Alcohol has chewed me up and spit me out," he rambled. "I'm hopeless." For some reason, it wasn't hard for Ethan to pour out what was continually running through his mind to Hope.

He watched as Hope took her mug to the sink and rinsed it. "Ethan, you are most definitely not hopeless. Before Saul was converted to Paul, he was a wicked man. He even tortured and killed Christians. But later, Saul had a change of heart. He accepted Jesus into his heart. Saul turned opposite from his ways, was changed to Paul and he didn't dare look back, because there was nothing there for him in the past. That story provides a hope for us that when it feels like we've gone too far for any way out, God provides a way of escape. He molds us into the person He wants us to be. Job 11:15 shows there *is* hope."

Ethan remained silent, not knowing how to reply to a girl who clearly made her case. He remembered the story of Paul. Paul was a great man, with an evil past. It was something Ethan could relate to.

"Hear me out. Why not start by getting rid of the temptation…by simply not buying the alcohol anymore?" Hope suggested. "And for every time you pass a bar whilst driving and can feel the desire burning in your throat, speed up and pass it by. My brother's a cop, I'll be sure to wave the tickets. It's for a worthy cause."

Ethan snorted. He was thankful for her subtle humor. The suggestion wasn't bad, but his heart wrestled with his mind. Could he really attempt to give up what felt so good? His head told him no, while his heart told him to give it a try. He had to at least start with not allowing the temptation within his household. "Help me pour the rest of my bottles down the drain." He settled the decision before he had more time to contemplate.

Ethan watched a smile tug at the corners of Hope's mouth. "I'm proud of you Ethan."

He began to grab numerous bottles and cans from his fridge. "You've been good for me Hope. I really appreciate you." Ethan's head began to thump as morning dawned. He glanced at the clock on the stove, 5:15 A.M. Hope was going to have to leave shortly to get the bakery ready to open.

A smile grew on Hope's face as she gladly poured the liquid down the sink drain. "Although you may not realize it, you're a good friend, Ethan. I really wish you'd consider your thoughts on God again, though. I don't mean to pry at you, but Jesus has given me a peace and hope that I can't receive anywhere else in this world. I'm here to share and inspire others with His love. Without any of that, my life itself would be depressing." She grabbed a whiskey bottle to pour next.

She was concerned about him, maybe too concerned, but Ethan let her continue. "I'll end the discussion of the matter with this: I want you to read the book of Job and then tell me what you think. Just read it and think about it. That's all I ask."

It wasn't a bad request, but that meant he would be cracking open a Bible again and pondering on it. Did he really want to risk doing that? "I'll do it." He abruptly promised her.

"I think it'll help your perspective," she responded with a confident smile.

They finished pouring out the last of the alcohol. To Ethan, it symbolized him putting away the foolish things. Putting this addiction behind him. This time he needed to fix himself. Ethan grabbed a garbage bag from underneath the sink and Hope stuffed the empty cans and bottles in the durable black bag.

"Are you free the Friday after Thanksgiving?" Hope spoke after cleaning up the counters in his kitchen.

"I'm free pretty much every day." He shrugged, leaning against the counter.

"Good, because after I'm done shopping my heart out with the girls, you and I are going Christmas tree shopping. Your house is screaming for some Christmas Spirit." She narrowed her brows.

"Bah. Humbug!" Ethan snarled his nose, knowing that this time of year just wasn't the same without his parents. They were the ones who made it special in the first place.

"Don't be such a Scrooge." Hope ruffled his hair. "Now, I've got thirty minutes until I need to leave to get the bakery opened up. You're about to get grilled with more questions. I must get to know you better." She held her nose in the air as she attempted to speak like a fancy British woman.

Ethan chuckled, watching Hope find the tea bags tucked away in a cabinet, making herself at home. When was the last time he'd felt wanted? The last time he'd genuinely communicated to a friend? He couldn't recall the last time. But a warm feeling settled in his heart, telling him he'd never feel alone again.

nine

He ate ramen noodles with siracha sauce. Ethan wasn't picky about movie selections, unless it was sci-fi…he made his point about hating sci-fi movies. His favorite color was green, and he loved when he used to coach the high school soccer team. Hope made a mental note to talk to the high school or middle school staff about possibly working him in as a coach or an assistant for the upcoming season of spring soccer. Owning a bakery had its perks; she knew who she needed to speak with about getting Ethan a position. He needed something to do with his time.

Not only had Ethan opened up this morning, but he'd welcomed her into his shattered life. It encouraged Hope's heart because maybe, just maybe, this was the first step that would lead him to God.

He was abused. Hope shuddered at the thought. Ethan's birth father had not been much of a father at all. She couldn't imagine the fear that rocked him to sleep as a child. It would have been like bugs crawling on her skin. Then to lose the happiness provided by Nathaniel and Kate, it would have turned Hope's world upside down.

God, everywhere Ethan turns, he's swallowed up by his unpleasant past. Help him to remember when You provided for him in the past. Help him to recall the good memories. He's trying to recover, he really is, but I'm afraid without You he'll eventually give back into the temptations. He needs You in order to put his abusive father in the past. He needs You to put the horrific way his stepdad and mom died in the past. Help him to realize that You extend a brighter future in the palm of Your hand.

She would pray for him and would continue to be there by his side. It was Hope's first instinct, and Ethan needed it.

Hope tried to focus back on her task at hand. She hummed as she piped buttery vanilla frosting onto a birthday cake for a three-year old. It was Wednesday, her last day in the bakery for the rest of the week. Containing her excitement for the weekend wasn't possible. Thursday would be Thanksgiving, which would mean eating loads of turkey with stuffing, and pumpkin pie cupcakes, of course. Friday would be shopping till she dropped with her mom, sister, and Sara. Then that evening she would go Christmas tree shopping with Ethan.

Contradictory to the café, where many orders were taking place at the counter, the kitchen was rather calm today. Everyone seemed to be working intently at their stations with their designated jobs for the day. In the corner of the rather large kitchen, two gigantic stainless-steel refrigerators were filled with desserts to either be delivered or picked up. Stacked convection ovens were directly across from the fridges, the aroma of pumpkin spice emanating from them.

"I'm going to get my hands on those Christian Louboutin shoes if I have to ride a battery-operated wheelchair and move people out of my way." Brianna perched herself on a counter, flipping through the Black Friday catalog.

"I recall someone sprinting to Ulta for a makeup palette on sale last year. It was the fastest I'd ever seen you run. You'll be just as fast on foot." Hope laughed at the memory of her sister rushing around in Ulta.

"In my defense, the palette was originally sixty bucks and I got it for sixteen dollars instead. I got a good deal." Brianna shrugged, her blonde ponytail whooshing behind her.

"Aren't you supposed to be baking pumpkin pies?" Hope's sister had the attention span of a squirrel.

"They're in the oven, thank you very much." Bri spoke matter-of-factly.

"In that case, I'm looking for a Kitchen-Aid mixer for my apartment. It's on sale, and it's pastel." Hope set her empty piping bag down and started in with the sprinkles.

"Right up your alley." The timer went off, and Bri hopped off the counter to get the pies out of the oven.

"The pumpkin cream cheese cupcake order has been taken care of!" One of the new employees, Jade, walked past Hope with a box of freshly made cupcakes.

"Bless you. They smell delicious!" Hope blew her a kiss.

Jade pretended to catch it and she giggled.

Hiring more people for Funfetti Café and Bakery had been the best decision Hope made for her bakery. Like separate ingredients in a recipe, the expanded group combined each of their talents and worked efficiently together, creating a glorious product. Things were getting accomplished faster, and Hope was finding herself with more time to breathe.

Hope dusted her hands off on her apron. "What do you think, Bri?" She took a step back to survey the cake.

Bri maneuvered her way from the fridge where she was putting pumpkin pies inside to cool. She squealed when she stopped at Hope's work station. "Hope, it's so cute! I love the watercolor base. It makes the whipped icing around the top of the cake stand out."

"Good." Hope nodded her head. Her sister's approval was always important to her.

As Hope placed the cake in a box and headed toward the fridge, the door separating the kitchen from the café swung open.

Laney, the young cashier on duty, entered with a smile that could melt a guy's heart. "Hope, there's a man out here asking for you." She tossed her slick, black hair off her shoulder.

"I wonder who that could be?" Bri hummed sarcastically.

If Hope hadn't been surrounded by a crowd, she would have wacked her sister. "Box my cake up and put it in the fridge." She opted for throwing a dish towel at Brianna instead. "Oh and...hush up." Hope heard Bri giggle as she walked away.

Hope could place a bet on who was asking for her, but betting wasn't very ladylike *or* Christian-like. She washed her hands in the deep metal sink by the door, then entered the café.

The tall and wide floor to ceiling windows left perfect natural lighting to flood the entire café full of white, pastel pink, and mint paint. Outside, fluffy snow fell gently from the sky, creating a picture-perfect moment, especially with the cute Edison lights strung from the ceiling.

Winter was coming.

People sat in booths, chattering amongst one another whilst sipping on hot coffee. Lines zig-zagged from the counter to the front door. Afternoons were their busiest time of day, but no one seemed to be annoyed or frustrated by the fact that the café was bustling. Everyone wore smiles upon their faces. That was the wonderful thing about Alton, everyone seemed to know everybody. The town was not too big, yet not too small. She was welcomed by many as she maneuvered her way through the crowd of people. Hope smiled as she found the person she figured she was looking for.

"You're becoming quite famous around Illinois." Ethan grinned.

He looked good this morning. He was dressed in a cashmere sweater that Hope would've loved to cuddle up to. His natural, wavy brown hair was swept back, and his eyes were glistening. He wore a smile that looked like it didn't have to be forced. Hope could fall in love with *this* Ethan and his cute dimples.

Where did that come from?

She shook herself from her thoughts. "I don't like the word famous." Hope walked around the counter of displayed desserts to meet him in a booth.

He had switched to a new spot.

She smiled at the miniscule things, for it was clear that Ethan was gradually changing.

"Hmm. Then…" He searched for an innovative word. "*Well-known.*"

"Better." Hope chuckled. "What can I get you this afternoon, Ethan?"

"Well, Sara and I are doing Thanksgiving this year, and I'm in charge of dessert and stuffing. I've got the stuffing under control, but I need some desperate help with dessert." The petrified look painted on his face caused Hope to bite her lip in attempt to suppress a chuckle.

"So, you're a homemade stuffing kind of guy, but you can't make a pumpkin pie?"

"If you consider Stove Top homemade, then yes." He grinned smugly.

Laughter erupted from Hope's belly. "What kind of dessert do you want?"

"Please no pumpkin pie. I've heard so much about it that I'm already sick of it." He took a sip from his coffee cup.

"I'll make a mental note of that." She glanced out the window, trying to think of a different dessert. Fluffier white flakes were falling from the grey sky now. "What about an apple streusel bread? I haven't made it in a while. It's not even on the menu right now, and apples are an appropriate alternative."

"Anything sounds better than pumpkin at the moment," he agreed, nodding.

She picked at her sweater sleeve as silence weaved its way into their conversation. She knew what she wanted to ask him but was afraid of his answer. Was now the right time? *When would be the "right" time?* Hope mentally rolled her eyes at herself as she braced herself to ask what God had put on her heart.

"Bri and I are taking cupcakes to our youth class at church tonight. We're going to let the kids decorate them as turkeys with candy pieces for Thanksgiving after their lesson." She chuckled. "It might be a messy mistake."

"I'm already envisioning frosting everywhere." He laughed and sat his cup of coffee down on the table.

"I'm going to recruit your sister to help. She's too polite to decline my request." Hope had already mentioned it to Sara briefly. She laughed as the image of Sara's eyes bulging out of her head reappeared in Hope's memory. Sara wasn't backing out of this task. No, ma'am. She needed something fun to do after all that she had been through recently.

"Put her in charge of the frosting." Ethan's sly grin told Hope all she needed to know about Sara and Ethan's relationship as brother and sister.

"I could put *you* in charge of the frosting if you came." Hope would enjoy herself even more if Ethan came. She prayed he would consider the inuendo she'd slipped on him.

Hope watched him wrestle the topic as he writhed in embarrassment. He slowly turned his smile into a frown, then shook his head. "I don't know."

She didn't want to push the subject if he already had his mind made up, but something inside her told her to offer once more. "It's just kiddos. The most they will do is pick their boogers and wipe them on you."

He laughed, letting crinkles form by his eyes. "That's promising."

Ethan felt out of place tonight helping Hope, her sister, and his own sister. He was an alcoholic, granted trying to sober up, but he was participating in church activities when he didn't even believe in God himself. He should've stayed home. He looked like the biggest hypocrite of all time. What seemed like a big classroom was now closing in around him

He had to admit, it was kind of exciting though—to be a part of something and feel wanted once again. The parents that dropped their kids off, had welcomed him politely without sending him any questioning second glances.

He focused in on Hope sharing the story of Jesus dying at Calvary for man's sin. How they should be thankful for Jesus making a way to God. She made the story exciting, leaving hope as she told how Jesus arose three days later. Her eyes sparkled, and Ethan noticed five minutes into the class that she was in her element. The group of kids were circled around her on the round orange mat in the middle of the classroom. Her smile lit up the entire room. She was dressed in an olive sweater that made her emerald eyes pop, and a mustard wool knit scarf around her neck. She was beautiful, and Ethan noticed that he was beginning to *like* her. He couldn't dare break a heart like hers when he wasn't a Christian. She wouldn't date someone who didn't believe.

The kids seemed to be intrigued, for she made the story come alive. She explained the Bible account down to their level of understanding but she didn't leave out a single thing.

It was so simple that even a child could understand, yet here Ethan was sitting in doubt and disbelief. Did he not believe, or was he too much of a coward to trust God again?

He considered the question that he tossed at himself. Ethan knew the answer deep down inside; he just didn't want to admit it. He shifted in his seat to get more comfortable, if that were even possible.

Sara took a seat beside of him at one of the tables. She smiled at him and he smiled back. His sister and Brianna had been preparing stations for each step of the decorating process. Sara would be at a table helping with plates, Bri and Hope would be at a station doing the frosting, and somehow Ethan had managed to get the position of decorating the turkey faces with chocolate candy pieces. If they weren't pretty, at least they'd still taste good.

"Do we have any prayer requests before we go to prayer?" Hope's sister sat down on the mat with the children after Hope finished the lesson.

Many kids mentioned their pets, some friends, and a frog named Ribbit who had hopped in the road in front of a car back in the early fall. Ethan and Sara chuckled at that last one.

A quiet boy in the corner with straight black hair whispered, "Pray for my daddy. Mommy says he drinks too much."

Ethan and Sara both froze. Memories hit too close for comfort. Images popped up left and right in Ethan's head, quicker than he could take a breath. His mind flashed back to a time when Peter slapped Kate across the face when she politely asked him to join them at church. His mom was too nice. She only wanted to see her husband in church. She'd held too much hope for Peter.

Another flashback hovered his brain. Peter had been too drunk to even recognize his own name and pointed a gun at Sara, so close to pulling to trigger. Ethan could almost hear the screams. He wanted the horrific incessant memories in his ears to stop, but they insisted on running ninety miles per hour.

The last memory would forever be embedded in his mind. Peter bellowed on his drunk lips that Ethan would never amount to anything. He remembered his birth father chucking his stuffed animal across the room as Ethan crawled to his bed for safety. It wasn't the cruelest thing Peter had done to Ethan, but it was the words that scarred the most. His mind seemed to be mutilated for life.

Ethan wanted to be more than just a speck of dirt. He wanted to prove the words of his birth father wrong. He deeply desired to be more than Peter ever was.

Would I, though?

His mind shifted to how much he drank in the past, and just recently. For the first time, Ethan realized he was making progress. He hadn't touched a bottle in quite some time. He had to do better. He just had to. He couldn't imagine scaring the daylights out of his own child one day.

He watched as Hope shifted her gaze to Ethan with a look of empathy. By the look on her face, she knew how hard the child's prayer request had hit Ethan. She glanced back down to the saddened child. Children were honest. Ethan found himself wanting to engulf the kid in a hug and never let go. He knew what it was like to not have a father.

Sara grabbed Ethan's hand and he squeezed it for comfort. She knew it hurt him, and without a doubt, he was sure it cut her just as deep.

Hope gave the little boy a hug that he very much needed. She reluctantly let go and they went to prayer. Ethan closed his eyes. He wouldn't pray, but he would at least be respectful.

"That's enough frosting, Brian." Hope attempted to be stern as the kid with spiky blonde hair grinned mischievously.

He wasn't going to stop.

Brian wasn't normally this ornery. Granted, he was spoiled, but he'd always been a decent kid in her and Bri's class. Maybe decorating cupcakes with five-year-

159

old kids wasn't the brightest idea she'd had in all her teaching years.

Hope drew out a breath as Brian squeezed the piping bag full of vanilla icing harder. "Brian, if you don't stop soon, that bag is going to—"

And suddenly, all that was in Hope's peripheral vision was fluffy white icing...everywhere.

"Pop." She sighed, finishing her statement even if it was too late.

Hope watched as Bri's mouth flung open and Ethan and Sara turned their heads at the sudden commotion. They covered their mouths with their hands, but she could visibly see them all doubling over in laughter. Icing had exploded on the table, on Brian's clothes, and all over Hope.

She closed her eyes and took a few deep breaths, flexing her fingers into her palms. The sticky icing could wait. Right now, the Lord was testing her patience and she needed a few seconds.

The boy stood there petrified, afraid he might get in trouble for not listening, but

Hope could hear the giggle trying to rumble in the kid's throat.

"Go decorate your cupcake with Ethan, now. You little rascal." Hope eventually spoke through gritted teeth. She tried to put on a grin to reassure Brian that he wasn't in trouble. Kids would only be kids for so long. *Let him have his fun.* Hope repeated the phrase in her head a couple jillion times.

Hope began her cleanup duty by sucking icing out of her hair. So much for her dignity and appearance. They were both long gone. "I'm not going to be able to get that out with a rag, am I?" Hope tugged at her sweater that now had icing smushed in between threads. She directed her question to her sister, who had been surprisingly quiet.

"You're going to need a new shirt." Brianna laughed with a shake of her head. "Remind me why we thought this was a good idea again?"

Hope had seriously wondered the same thing, but as she tilted her head and watched the group around her, she discovered the reason why. While for a brief minute it might have been chaotic, the brightly lit expressions on the children's faces made it worth it. After they'd said grace, most were now chomping down on cupcakes and giggling at each other's decorations.

"Because of that," she replied. Hope nodded toward Ethan and a group full of kids surrounding him. Ethan shared a laugh with a kid who decided it was way cooler to make a cow than a turkey.

"He's having a lot of fun." Sara bagged up paper plates since the line had officially come to an end.

"I can agree." Hope watched Ethan with a genuine smile as he helped the kids. His emerald eyes were sparkling tonight. She'd been worried that he wouldn't like being around children but watching him hold their hands or try to make them laugh when they were sad, proved her worries wrong. He truly would make a great father one day, especially if he gave God room to work in his heart.

Ethan noticed her eyes that were fixated on him and she looked away quickly before she could blush. She could already sense his smirk. He finished helping the last ones in the line and directed them to their seats, then walked over to join the girls.

"They must be enjoying them." Bri laughed. All the kids were silent as icing smothered the edges of their mouths.

"Who wouldn't love your guys' cupcakes?" Ethan grabbed an extra one for himself. "I happen to think Hope's the best baker in the world."

"You're subtly flirting, Ethan." Bri's cunning grin earned a kick from Hope.

"Put a sock in it, Bri," Hope muttered, sending a death glare her sister's way.

"Come on, Brianna. You and I should make for sure the kids have enough napkins." Sara linked her arm in Brianna's.

Hope owed Sara one. Her sister didn't know when to be quiet. It could be amusing at times…just not this time. She watched as the two walked away. "My sister is embarrassing." Hope still clutched the piping bag she'd snatched from Brian.

"But you love her." Ethan grinned.

Hope threw away the piping bag after she removed the coupler and tip. "She's my sister, I have to," she teased, causing the both of them to laugh.

"I must say, you still look lovely even with frosting caked in your hair." He grabbed a strand of her frizzy hair and gently pulled some icing out.

Both the comment and gesture made her cheeks light on fire. "It's going to take forever to wash out." She picked at a few clumps of icing on her sweater.

He continued to help her get it out of her tangled hair. Hope smiled, finding this Ethan adorable. "The kid said he wanted to add candy to your hair...and give you an apron." Ethan's comment caused her to laugh.

"I don't know whether to feel flattered or offended."

"A pretty woman like you would look just as adorable with M&M's in her hair as she would without. I mean, the icing isn't so bad." He spoke sarcastically, but she could hear the seriousness that lay beyond his comment.

Hope could tell Ethan was trying to be gentle with her hair, but he pulled a little too hard this time, causing her to wince. "Trying to make me bald while we're at it?"

"Sorry, there's a huge chunk of icing on your right side." He apologized and gave up working on the knotted strands of hair around the icing.

Her gaze met his as he removed his hand from her hair. The look they exchanged between each other seemed different this time. Hope watched his sparkling eyes shift from her eyes to her lips, then back to her eyes again. Hope's heartbeat fluttered at the startling realization that Ethan wanted to kiss her. But Ethan quickly pulled himself back, restraining his lips from touching hers. Hope found herself immediately relaxing. It was a decision made well for the both of them. She couldn't get herself tangled in something more than a friendship when she knew Ethan's heart wasn't right with the Lord.

Hope tried to make the moment less embarrassing for Ethan and his temptation. "I'd love some help cleaning the sticky table." She gestured toward the table coated with vanilla icing that was beginning to melt the longer it sat there.

Ethan cleared his throat, looking everywhere but directly at Hope. "Sure."

ten

Ethan placed the leftover plate of cupcakes on his kitchen island. He smiled at one cupcake that looked like a decent turkey. The little boy who spoke about his father during prayer requests had clung to Ethan the entire evening—Colin. The kid liked *Star Wars* and puppies. Hope had mentioned after the evening was over that Colin's father was also taking counseling sessions with Mark for alcohol, but he was failing to let go of the bottles of poison.

The evening had been fun, as a matter of fact, it had been the most enjoyable day he'd had in a long time. The image of frosting smushed in Hope's hair lingered in his mind. Ethan had wanted to kiss her, but he would have made a terrible mistake if he would have followed through. Hope deserved someone so much better than himself.

Hope promised she would call him later tonight, and Ethan was holding onto that promise. He was beginning to realize how much Hope was meaning to him. For the first time in a long time, he reckoned he could almost say he had a friend. That recognition settled well in the depths of his heart.

Ethan strolled past the living room, not bothering to turn on any lights, and headed up the whitewashed staircase to his bedroom. He entered his bedroom and flipped the light switch on. For a moment, he stood still at the wooden frame of his door and turned the light back off. He stared a moment into the depths of darkness, then turned the light back on. The bright lights swallowed up the dark room that seemed so chilling.

It finally clicked. That's how his life had been as a child...so dark and petrifying. However, when Nathaniel had introduced Ethan to Jesus, it was like a brand new, bright world. Ethan's life had been changed and completely rearranged for the better. But after losing his mom and stepdad, his faith had been like a candle blown out from the slightest bit of wind.

Should I turn the Light Switch to my life back on?

Ethan pivoted back out of his bedroom as his feet led him farther down the hall to a large master bedroom on the end. His bottom lip began to quiver at the realization of what he was about to do. He paused and took a deep breath. Slowly, he twisted the black knob open and took in his surroundings. Tears automatically dammed up in his eyes. Ethan attempted to straighten his back and square his shoulders. He wouldn't let himself cry. He needed to be a man.

The entire farmhouse and property had been Nathaniel's. When Nathan and Ethan's mom got married, this was the house his family had moved into. It had become a home instantly. Ethan used to ride his stepdad's horses across the acres of fields they owned. Nathan taught Ethan how to properly kick a soccer ball in their backyard.

And there were countless times Ethan would sit on his mom's lap underneath the pergola and watch the stars at night. The farmhouse represented a change…a fresh start.

It was in his parent's will for Ethan to inherit it all if something ever happened to them, since Sara had inherited their grandparent's place. Ethan never thought much of it, for he figured he would never have to lose his parents at the early age he did. He assumed one day he would be able to visit his parents' place with his children and tell them stories of the things he did while he was a child. He supposed his kids would one day get to spend the night with their grandparents and sit under the stars as he once did.

He'd been wrong.

Once they lost their parents, Sara was quick to move out. She couldn't stand the thought of living in the house without their mother. Ethan could never muster the courage to move out, for he felt like his purpose was to be here, where memories still lingered. Although, he had let the bad memories overpower the good ones, and soon let himself sip on a beer to dissolve his tears.

Ethan lost control ever since—bar hopping, drunk driving, and whiskey tasting. The true joy wasn't there anymore. He let his life and dignity crumble right between his own fingers.

What would my parents think of me now?

He was too ashamed to even try to think of the pain it would cause them to see him in this pitiful condition.

Ethan rarely entered the bedroom full of so many memories. It always caused him discomfort in too many ways to count.

His mom's peach quilt that she had sewn on her own was still spread across the bed, wrinkle free. The picture frame holding a picture of the family on his stepdad's nightstand was still tilted to where Nathaniel would have seen it when he would wake in the mornings. His mom's vanity still held her jewelry, perfumes, and makeup. And the window seat still held one of Dee Henderson's novels. His mom loved to read.

Everything was just as his parents had left it. It was like stepping back into time. He expected to see his stepdad come whistling through the door at any given moment.

He crept toward his mom's bedside table. Her violet leather Bible still lay in the same place she kept it for years. Instead of running for alcohol at the overwhelming memories this time, he was drawn toward the torn, well-used Bible that remained untouched since his mom passed.

Ethan gingerly picked the Bible up and took a seat by the window. Light snow drops were continuing to fall from the sky, creating a white fluffy blanket on the green grass. Ethan carefully turned the pages of his mother's Bible to the book of Job. Even if it had been three years since he cracked open a Bible, it was still familiar—like he never left it.

The margins of his mother's Bible were filled with colorful notes. He smiled at one of her notes on a sermon, her *i*'s were dotted with hearts. Ethan found the first chapter and wiped his sweaty palms on his pants. He began to read.

"He felt uncomfortable, Sara." Hope transferred the shopping bag handles from her right wrist to her left one as she looked over the chalkboard menu. She ordered a hot tea for herself and a coffee for her mom and sister, then let Sara order hers.

The conversation topic had become a normal one between Sara and Hope...Ethan. Hope hadn't expected Colin to speak about his alcoholic father Wednesday night. She noticed the way Ethan shifted uncomfortably at the prayer request. The look on his face had been unbearable for Hope. Ethan and Sara had both been through a terrible past, and Hope knew to see someone else going through something similar sparked those memories back to life in a different way for them.

When she called Ethan that night, he was reading the Bible—something that should have surprised Hope, but instead, it didn't. Hope could only pray that Ethan was under conviction. She knew he was looking for a way out, and Jesus was the only way. If being convicted meant that it would eventually bring Ethan eternal peace, then she would continue to pray for it.

Hope exchanged her cash for the travel carton of three coffees and one tea that the barista handed her. "Thank you." Hope smiled and started to walk back to the table her mom and Bri were waiting at.

"Good. He needs to know he's missing out on something only God can supply." Ethan's sister strolled by Hope's side.

The mall was crowded and fully decked out in Christmas decorations now that Thanksgiving was officially over. Hope's claustrophobia had been put to the test today as the mall was elbow to elbow full of people. Black Friday's were getting more intense with each year, and Hope was beginning to wonder if the sales were worth all the stress and madness.

Hope considered Sara's statement.

"There's no need to feel bad, Hope. He needed the gentle shove. He needed someone to help him realize he *could* have a brighter future." Sara smiled at Hope, reassuring her it was okay. "If he didn't feel convicted, then you would have been too nice. There's a difference between being a caring friend and being a nosy no one."

173

"I haven't known you for long, but goodness gracious you're a great friend!" Hope threw her arm full of shopping bags around Sara's shoulder.

Hope pulled out a chair beside Bri as they approached the group. She set her bags down beside of her on the floor, and then handed everyone their hot beverages.

"What would I do without coffee?" Bri took a whiff of her hot drink before taking a sip.

"You'd survive." Their mom patted Brianna on the back.

Hope drummed her fingers on the table. "So, have we got what we came here for?"

"My babies are safely in my possession, so yes." Brianna patted her Christian Louboutin bag and tossed her long hair over her shoulder. "Besides, you just want to leave us lovely girls to have more time to hang out with Ethan." Bri dramatically rolled her eyes, but it was obvious she was only teasing.

Hope kicked Bri under the table with her boots. She didn't want to admit it to her sister because she would never hear the end of it. Truth was, Ethan was growing on Hope quite a bit. "He's better company than you." Hope stuck her tongue out at her little sister.

"Are you two twelve or adults?" Heather's eyes narrowed at her daughters, then she took a drink of her macchiato.

Hope chuckled at her mom's question; it was rhetorical...definitely rhetorical.

"I actually need your guys' help." Hope placed her scalding hot tea on the table. She had a plan, and she was going to follow through by making this Christmas the best one Ethan had experienced in many years.

Sara's left eyebrow perked up over her coffee cup as she noted Hope's sudden change in conversation.

"I want to make this Christmas one that Ethan will never forget."

Hope had arrived at the Christmas tree farm thirty minutes ago. Her mom, Bri, and Sara were all heading back to Ethan's place to decorate it inside and out. Sara mentioned there were two tubs full of old Christmas decorations in his shed. They also picked up colorful lights and a few blowup decorations for outside while they were still in the mall.

Ethan's place was in desperate need of a Christmas makeover, and Hope couldn't wait to see how surprised he would be. Hope figured on keeping him distracted by picking out a tree until she got a text of approval from her sister that they were done throwing up Christmas on Ethan's home. Then, Hope and Ethan would bring the tree back home for the two of them to decorate. The plan was going well so far.

"How was your Thanksgiving? Sara mentioned the apple bread was tasty." Hope watched a smile grow across his face and she couldn't contain the warmth that filled her from her shivering fingers all the way to her toes. Who knew dimples could do that to a woman?

"It was *actually* nice. Sara and I spent the afternoon watching movies and playing battleship—which by the way, Sara likes to cheat at." He stopped at a large pine tree to examine it, then moved on to another one. "Yours?"

"Mom made a wonderful dinner. She stuffed us all full of turkey and sent us home after a very intense Scrabble game." Hope chuckled as she flashbacked to her brother's face full of amusement when he'd "beat" everyone. Truth was, everyone was getting sick of his Scrabble tactics and secretly agreed to let him win.

"I've never known Scrabble to be such a heated game before." He laughed as he walked down the path of different sized pine trees.

Hope breathed in the crisp, piney aroma that smelled exactly like Christmas. "Then you'll have to join my family sometime and discover for yourself." Hope meant it too. It would be good for Ethan to have a family around him.

He smiled. "What about this one?"

Hope took a step back to inspect the tree Ethan had been looking at. The fragrant needles were full, and a few pinecones spritzed in a cinnamon scent were still attached. It was a beautiful tree with snow lightly dusted on it from a few hours earlier. "It's tall, fluffy, and gorgeous."

"Checks off all the boxes. I think she's the one." Hope grinned at how excited Ethan seemed to be about something so little.

"Cut the pretty thing down, and I'll buy us some hot chocolate. Then, you can take me to your place. I want to help decorate." She put her red beanie back on her head to cover her cold ears.

"Sounds good. My fingers are frozen and if mine are, I'm sure yours are." Ethan handed her cash. "I like whipped cream, and lots of it." He grinned.

"I'll remember that." Hope weaved her way through the maze of Christmas trees to a small shack selling hot chocolate. She ordered two to go, one with loads of marshmallows, and the other with extra whipped cream. While she was there, she went ahead and paid for the tree as well.

Hope smiled to herself as she gripped the two steaming cups full of cocoa. She was enjoying her time spent with Ethan. He seemed relaxed and mellow today, something Hope sensed was the way he used to be. He'd gone three weeks without alcohol so far, and the tremendous improvement in his actions was beginning to show. He was open to subjects that he used to be private about. He'd willingly talk to her about his parents. Hope was beginning to see a spark in him that hadn't been there before…an earnest desire to do better.

"One hot chocolate for you, and one for me." Hope handed Ethan the warm cup of chocolate when she made her way back to him.

He shivered as he took the cup. "C'mon, let's head back to my place and get warm. I'll bring you back here to get your car later this evening."

Hope bit her lip. Her sister hadn't texted yet. "Do you care to take me to the library first? I need a new book to read tonight." It was true, but she was mainly stalling for time.

Ethan agreed sweetly as he led her and the tree back to his truck. All the while, Hope prayed that her sister, mom, and Sara could pull off the rest of the decorating in time.

Ethan pulled off the interstate, drove down the streets of Alton for a while, then turned on his signal as he drove up the winding dirt road that lead to his home. He was genuinely the happiest he had been in a long time, but something was still missing. There was a gap that needed to be filled.

He glanced to his right where Hope was sitting in silence in the passenger seat. She was concentrating on the back of her book that she borrowed from the library. He found the pout of her lips as she focused on something to be cute. She looked pretty today, but to him she was pretty every day. Her eyes twinkled, and her freckles added a uniqueness to her face that didn't need to be covered with makeup. Her blonde hair, tinted with a light red, was something that he had grown to love. She was effortlessly beautiful, and she didn't even know how many heads turned her way on a daily basis.

Hope made today a day that would not be easily forgotten. It was the simple gesture that had turned into so much more, and Ethan was thankful for that.

Ethan pulled in his driveway and a gasp escaped his lips. "What's all this?" He kept his hand on the steering wheel whilst he stared his house down. He absorbed the home that almost looked unfamiliar to him now. It seemed to have life. Snowflake lights draped along the banister of his porch. Two giant snow globe inflatables sat on both sides of the wooden walkway up to his porch, one with Santa Claus in it and another with a snowman. Rainbow colored lights lined his windows, and festive Christmas wreaths were hung everywhere.

"Surprise!" He looked over at Hope whose smile glistened in the passenger's seat. He watched as her face waited for him to react.

"You didn't…" He let a small grin spread wide across his face as he looked back at his home.

"I really like it when you smile big enough for me to see your dimples." Hope distracted him as she chuckled at his facial expressions.

"How did you do it?" He was puzzled at how his house had been decorated from the time he had left to meet Hope, 'til now.

"Let's just say your sister said to stop hiding your key under the mat."

"Sara did this?"

Hope nodded. "Along with Bri and my mom."

Ethan had yet to meet Hope's mom, but he already loved her. He hopped out of his truck and ran to the passenger's side to open the door for Hope.

"I hope you don't mind your electricity bill going up for the next month." Hope smirked and grabbed onto his hand that he extended to help her out of his truck.

Ethan didn't reply. Instead, he simply wrapped his arms around her slender figure, engulfing her in a hug. Obviously shocked at the gesture, Hope held herself frozen for a few seconds, then she wrapped her arms around his neck and rested her head on his broad shoulders. "Thank you," he whispered against her neck. Ethan could drown in her flowery perfume.

He didn't know how she had it arranged, and frankly didn't care. Hope had shown how much she cared for him through her actions, and that was appreciated more than words could describe. Hope was becoming more important to him daily, and the more she cared for him, the more he fell for her.

"I hope you like it." Hope smiled as Ethan pulled away from the hug.

"I absolutely love it." He grinned at her, then studied his home. "Let's get the tree inside."

"Good idea." She followed behind him up the porch steps after he unloaded the tree. She paused at the door before she unlocked it for him. "Before I unlock your house, be prepared for more."

He laughed. "There's more?"

"Go big or go home, am I right?" Hope opened the door as he cautiously walked inside.

"There are Christmas bulbs and lights everywhere!" He giggled like a kid as he carried the tree from the entryway to his spacious living room.

Ethan felt like he was on the brink of tears as he soaked in each detail. He spotted his mother's Christmas throw strewn across the couch, along with festive pillows. Jars were filled with fake snow and car trinkets on side tables. Lining the bottom of his fireplace, the old houses that him and his stepfather used to play with were lit up, creating a Christmas village. It all hit him like a wave, but the memories didn't choke him...this time they flooded his mind with joy.

"My mom likes to decorate." Hope laughed and helped him prop the tree against one of the four corners in the living room.

Ethan grinned. "I'll have to thank her." He put his hands on his hips and studied his living room. "Put the tree in the corner by the fireplace that now has frosted berry garland on the mantle, *or* move the couch to face the windows and put the tree in the center of the windows? That's the real question."

Hope chuckled. "By the windows." She confirmed what he initially wanted, but Ethan also desired her opinion, for some reason it mattered. The tree would be a sight in front of the floor to ceiling windows, especially since their sisters and Heather had strung evergreen berry garland around them too.

"I think so too." Ethan picked up the pine tree, leaving trails of pine needles behind him. "This is messy."

"Maybe, but it's worth it." Hope grinned and pulled her hair up in a ponytail before she helped him move the leather couch. "Your sister texted. She left the tree decorations sitting on the kitchen table. I'll go get them."

He smiled as he watched her walk away and disappear into his kitchen. She was getting prettier by the minute. He was going to enjoy the rest of the evening with her. Ethan shook his head and grabbed the tree stand and a drill. Best to get to work and not to let his mind wander.

A few minutes later she come back dangling two large bags. "Got them!"

"The tree is set up and ready for decorations." Ethan stepped back to get a good look at the lush ten-foot pine. It was stunning in front of the large farmhouse windows.

"What's this?"

Ethan turned around to see Hope studying something on his glass coffee table.

He made his way toward whatever had attracted her attention. She read a note on top of what looked like his parent's old record player. He hadn't seen the thing in ages.

He sat down on the white fur rug beside of Hope. "Sara must have found it. My mom and stepdad used to dance in the living room to these old records." He smiled at the memory, even if there was a pang of sadness that came with it.

Hope smiled at him. "It's a good memory."

"Yes." He went through the pile of records, reading the titles. "We'll do the Charlie Brown hits." Ethan grinned.

"My favorite." Hope opened the briefcase style record player and Ethan placed the record in its designated place. "Mark's puppy is named after the dog on the show." She chuckled.

"I didn't know he liked animals." Ethan had become fond of Hope's older brother. The counselling sessions were helping Ethan grow, and Mark was becoming a good friend.

186

"He's a sucker for them." Hope placed the needle on the record and it began to play a Christmas carol.

"I'll have to remember that." He snickered. "Let's decorate." He pulled her to her feet and grabbed a bag of decorations.

"Look what I found." Hope held up red and white fuzzy stockings to show Ethan.

"Those used to be my parent's. Sara and I used to have the fun Rudolph ones."

Hope smiled at him, praying the reminiscence would be a good one. Ethan's grin made Hope relax.

He took the two stockings from her hands and hung them off the wooden mantle above the white stone fireplace. "One for you, and one for me." He beamed and continued where he left off with some tinsel.

"You're too kind. Sara is going to feel left out." Hope hung another white bulb on the tree.

"I think she'll be fine." A cunning grin formed across his face as he tossed the last handful of gold tinsel on the tree.

Hope took a step back. The tree was gorgeous. White lights made the glittered gold and white bulbs sparkle, and the shiny gold tinsel added a playful touch. "I'm jealous of your tree."

He laughed and tugged at the leftover tinsel garland wrapped around her neck. "Why is that?"

She took a seat on his comfy couch. "First of all, your tree is ten times bigger than mine...not cool *or* fair. Second, Bri came over after Thanksgiving and helped me decorate mine. She goes crazy with decorations. I'm not even sure if there's a tree underneath it all anymore." Hope chuckled. Her sister used too much different colored tinsel than Hope preferred.

"If it's any consolation, the tree's only up for a month." Ethan sneered and sat down in the handmade wooden rocking chair beside of the couch.

Hope yawned and rested her head on a comfortable pillow.

"You're getting tired." Ethan observed her facial expression, and Hope felt a helpless blush creep to her face.

She took a glance at the rose gold watch on her wrist. It was past eleven. She looked up and nodded at Ethan. "Take me home, Ethan." She'd have Bri swing by with her and get her car in the morning before work, for she was too exhausted to be behind the wheel.

He only nodded. Ethan got Hope on her feet and pulled her into a hug. His warm embrace welcomed her, along with his spicy cologne. Hope found herself burying her face in his sweatshirt before she could even think. She didn't even have to look up, she could sense the smile growing on Ethan's face. She needed him to trust in Jesus now more than ever, for she was falling for him.

"I've got a spare bedroom, you know." He pulled away to look into her tired eyes, but he kept his large hands on her shoulders.

Hope instantly shook her head, knowing it was a bad idea. She shifted her gaze to the floor. "I need to go home. Mark will be calling me."

189

FINDING HOPE

He nodded with a smile, accepting Hope's small protest and led her to his truck.

eleven

"I appreciate all that you've done. You've made today an evening I won't forget." Ethan put the truck in Park as he pulled up to Hope's apartment complex. She had fallen asleep on the ride over and was just now beginning to wake up. She was cute when she slept—both hands under her head and curled in a ball.

Hope yawned and ran her fingers through her hair. "At any other time of day, I'd come up with something sweet to say back, but I'm too tired. So...ditto." She unbuckled her seatbelt.

Ethan chuckled. "You're cute when you're sleepy."

He watched as Hope blushed and shook her head. "Don't pick my brain when I'm not fully functioning." Ethan heard the seriousness in her tone, but he also caught the slightest bit of humor.

"You're welcome, by the way. I haven't had this much fun in a while." Hope added to her previous comment with a sluggish grin.

That smile of hers was going to get him in trouble. "Neither have I." He fumbled with the keys that were still in ignition and watched small flurries of snow fall from the night sky. The flakes landed on the white, freshly coated ground.

Hope gathered her purse and coat. Putting tonight to an end was going to be hard when Ethan didn't want to be alone.

Just as she grabbed the truck door to open it, he caught her gaze and stopped her in her tracks. Ethan tucked away a loose strand of straight hair behind her ear and placed a gentle kiss on her lips. It was meant to be a simple thank you for all she had done.

After a few moments, Hope pulled her lips away with a shake of her head, but she left her forehead resting against his. Ethan immediately regretted what he had done as he watched her chin quiver and tears well up in her eyes. Her face displayed a hundred different mixed emotions, and Ethan's heart constricted at the fact that he had caused her pain.

"Ethan, you're going to break my heart." She removed her forehead from his and picked at the bracelet she was wearing. "I promised God I was going to wait on someone who cared more about Him than me. I know you mean well, and I know you care for me Ethan, but the simple fact that you're still wrestling with the decision to believe or not tells me that I can't do this. Not yet." She wiped a tear that fell from her eye. "Don't let what you physically want get in the way of what you spiritually need," Hope added.

Ethan's jaw locked. He didn't want to put Hope in this position. Here he was, about to lose someone who already meant so much to him, yet his own foolishness was getting in the way. *Stupid, stupid.*

"I've been reading Job." It was all he had to offer.

Hope stilled. After a few seconds of silence, she spoke. "It's a good book."

He stared straight ahead at the apartment building. "Full of faithfulness and trust." It still marveled Ethan how God would allow something so terrible to happen in someone's life. To see Job's reaction to the obstacles though…it was shocking. Job reacted with such grace and faithfulness toward God.

"God loves you, you know. What seems hard to you is making the first step." Hope pulled a ring of keys out of her bag.

Ethan took the comment in. He indeed was avoiding the first step.

God loved him.

He swallowed hard. If she didn't leave soon, she would see him cry, and he didn't want that again. She'd seen enough.

"Goodnight, Ethan." She opened the door and took one last look at him. The despairing look carved into her beautiful face was more than Ethan could handle. He'd taken a knife and twisted it in his own heart.

Ethan kept one hand on the wheel and tried his best to gain a voice. "Night, Hope."

Hope collapsed on her bed and buried her face in her pillow. She let the tears finally pour from her burning eyes.

Ethan had kissed her.

Letting that fact sink in made her head thump. It wasn't a bad kiss. As a matter of fact, she enjoyed the kiss. It was the guilt and shame after that told her not to get entangled in such a mess. Hope's heart felt like it was a thousand shards of glass that used to be a gorgeous cake display.

It wasn't that Ethan had a bad past. It wasn't that Ethan had only been sober for three weeks. It *was* the fact that he didn't serve God. The One who meant everything to her. What Hope feared most was beginning to take place in her life…falling for someone who didn't have their priorities straight.

God, why? I can't deny it. I like the man. Have I already gone too far? If not, should I turn around and get myself out now?

Her phone rang, interrupting her tear-filled prayer. Hope picked up the corded telephone on her nightstand and drew in a deep breath before answering. "Hello?"

"You're crying...what's wrong?" Her brother's worrisome tone came through the other end.

Hope rolled her eyes. She'd never been good at covering her emotions, and her brother could read her like the back of his hand. "I'm fine, Mark."

"If you don't tell me what the matter is within the next five seconds, I'm calling Bri and you can speak with her." His voice stood firm and strong. Mark was still in Chicago with their dad, or he would be the one marching through the town of Alton and barging through her apartment door in the middle of the night. So, of course he'd recruit Brianna if needed to take his position.

Hope sat up straight and rested her back on the wooden headboard to her bed. It wasn't worth the fight. "Ethan kissed me," she whispered, still not believing it herself. "We had such a good day—decorating his tree, singing along to Christmas music. Then, when he dropped me off at my house…he kissed me, and I kissed him back."

Mark's sigh carried through the other end of the receiver. Just the huff of his breath was enough to make Hope's shoulders slump. Though deep down in her heart, she desired to hear her brother's wise advice.

"Hope." His gentle voice paused. "I assume you like Ethan?"

For her, the answer was simple. "Yes."

"Do you care for Ethan?" This wasn't going the way she thought it would. Then again, when was the last time his advice went the way she imagined it?

"Of course, I do." She brought her knees into her chest and rested her chin on them.

"What about you? Do you care for yourself?"

The question he provoked her mind with made her head spin.

He spoke after she decided not to reply. "Hope, there's no doubt Ethan is changing. God is dealing with him, and I

197

think you helped open that door for him. But he's still fighting the fact that he needs a Savior, and until he realizes that he needs God, I'm afraid you're going to get hurt. As your older brother who has seen a lot, I don't want to watch you fall apart. Your faith is strong, Hope. I don't want to see it crumble because of an unbalanced relationship."

With the palm of her hand, Hope brushed tears away from her cheeks. "Then why does my faith feel weak at this very moment?" Her question wasn't one to smart her brother off, it was one she sincerely felt needed answered.

"You're trying to take the paintbrush from God's hands while He's still painting. In other words, you're stepping out before God's ready to reveal to you His plan. Give Him time. Don't be in a hurry. Until then, put your faith in Psalm 42:5," Mark replied.

She knew the passage by heart. *Why art thou cast down, O my soul? and why art thou disquieted in me? hope thou in God: for I shall yet praise him for the help of his countenance.*

"There's nothing wrong with simply being Ethan's friend, Hope. In fact, he's become quite a good friend to me. As a good friend though, you want the best for the opposite person. If not anything else, I would love to see Ethan get his life right again with God. But it can't be because we want him to, it must be on *his* own terms. He has to make the decision within himself. The Holy Spirit has to call him."

Hope understood. She really did want the best for Ethan, but also for herself. At this clear point, she saw nothing wrong with taking a step back, drawing a line, and just being Ethan's friend. She refused to desert him like almost everyone else in his life did. What kind of friend would she be?

"Are you okay?" Mark's gentle voice soothed her heart.

Hope loved her brother. "I will be." She pulled the white comforter up to her neck as chills rippled down her spine. "How was the Bears game with Dad?" She shifted the conversation to something she knew would excite her.

"Snowy and cold. We lost." He laughed. "Dad had an enjoyable time though. He ate three footlong corndogs, then stole my kettle corn that costed me five bucks."

Hope threw her head back in laughter. Her dad was an unforgettable character. "I can't wait to see pictures."

"There are at least fifteen selfies on my phone of Dad with his foam finger and Kool-Aid. He likes to steal phones now, so beware of the photobombing thief running lose in our family."

The laughter felt good and fed Hope deep down in her soul. "That crazy man is always up to something."

Ethan stared at the twinkling Christmas tree lights. His eyes watered from the way they stung.

He was alone now. Something about being alone brought out all his emotions, and tonight he was torn. He was positive Hope was much more broken than he was right now.

He hadn't been able to go to sleep after dropping her off at her apartment. So, here he was, two in the morning, staring at the Christmas tree they decorated earlier in the day. What had been a wonderful day, ended in a terrible mistake. Ethan sank even farther in the couch, trying to get comfortable. With a huff, he eventually rested his head on the armrest. Every time he closed his eyes, the image of Hope's anguished face after he kissed her appeared in his mind. Her crinkled eyebrows, and her eyes that lost their sparkle broke his heart. He made a mistake tonight and didn't know how to fix it.

Ethan groaned and buried his face in a throw pillow. He stressed to himself multiple times to not break her heart, and he ended up doing just that. He never wanted to be the reason behind someone's tears, and this night, he was the *only* reason.

He respected Hope's opinion about God, but he also knew respect wouldn't be enough. He had to truly believe that Jesus Christ was the Son of God for Hope to even consider him more than a friend. It was a challenge he didn't know if he was willing to face.

His mind wandered off to his stepdad and mother. They would want him going to church again. They would want him to be bubbling with joy. They *wouldn't* want him in this position. If they were here, they'd be doing everything they could to help Ethan out of the endless blackhole he seemed to be trapped in.

Ethan longed for hope beyond his own situations and despair. The only hope that he was searching for seemed to be in the God that Hope was fully putting her trust in.

Every reason for Ethan not to believe seemed distant tonight. Depression came with alcohol, and he no longer desired for that taste to confuse and consume him anymore. The only feeling left was the fear of being alone. Ethan didn't want that. More than anything, he didn't want his life to be empty. And that's how he felt tonight...empty.

twelve

Mark Lawson sat his Bible down on the desk in front of him and rubbed his temples. His last counseling session with Colin's father, Richard, hadn't gone well. Mark held on to high hopes that his session with Ethan would brighten his day. Ethan had immensely improved within their one month of counseling. He hadn't consumed any alcohol since the night he'd called Mark's sister, Hope. Mark saw improvement in Ethan, and he saw a person slowly bouncing back to life.

He skimmed once more through his notes and Bible before heading out to meet Ethan at his home today. As he drove toward Ethan's home, Mark tried his best to put himself in Ethan's shoes. He prayerfully asked God to give him the words he needed to help Ethan out. Mark couldn't even walk without Jesus holding his hand. How was Ethan doing it? He had to feel so alone without God to depend on.

Ethan simply needed Someone to rely on. Something to trust in...a hope beyond his life. Mark was determined to prove to Ethan today that his only hope would be found in a Man named Jesus.

Her head spinning in circles, Hope took a deep breath and tried to focus. She felt like she was going to throw up her lunch and the granola bar she'd munched on for breakfast. Two weeks until Christmas and she was getting sick. *Great.* She couldn't let that happen. She needed to be fully functionable at work during the busiest time of year for the bakery.

Funfetti Café and Bakery was swamped with orders today. Hope didn't feel much like putting icing on a cake, but orders were coming in left and right and Hope made her decision to push through. It wasn't a hard decision to make, for her heart and soul went into her bakery in the little town that had grown fond her desserts.

Hope pushed a fresh tray of snickerdoodle cookies into the oven. Once that was done, she sighed and let her back rest on the cool white concrete wall beside the oven. Closing her eyes, chills washed over her arms, and she sneezed another hundredth time.

"Hope that makes the seventh time you've sneezed in under two minutes. Get out of the bakery or I will call Mark, and you know he'll drag you out." Brianna stopped trimming fondant for a cake and removed her plastic gloves to feel Hope's forehead. "No one likes contaminated cupcakes."

"I'm fine. It's just a little cold." Hope shrugged, trying to shake it off, but her sister wouldn't buy it.

"You're sick—" Brianna snarled her nose as Hope sneezed again "—and spreading germs everywhere! You don't want your customers complaining. Go home and get some rest. If you're not feeling better in the morning, one of us will take you to the doctor." Brianna untied Hope's apron and exchanged it for Hope's coat. "Better yet, go visit the doctor on your way home."

"Who's going to get everything done?" Hope protested with a whine.

"You've got to remember that you have more staff now. We can handle this. If I need an extra set of hands, I'll call Sara and see what she's doing after work," Bri promised with a sympathetic look. "Besides, you're probably just lovesick. You and Ethan haven't seen each other in a while." Bri's sly grin appeared.

Hope had made the mistake of telling her younger sister about the kiss her and Ethan exchanged...the kiss that never should have happened. Bri hadn't let it go since, and it made it hard for Hope to shrug it off.

Hope snatched her purse and scarf from a hook by the back door, giving up the fight without much effort on her end at all. She needed to go home. "Maybe that's for a reason," Hope responded. She'd seen Ethan at the bakery now and then, but they hadn't had time to talk it out.

"Rest up, I need someone to tease while I'm hard at work." Bri patted Hope on the shoulder as Hope walked out the back door into the freezing winter weather.

The rest of her day was going to consist of cheesy Christmas romance movies and plenty of sleep.

Mark Lawson's POV

"There are some things that just do not come with an explanation, Ethan." He licked his dry lips. "Because I'm your friend and I care about you, I'm going to tell you this: I need you to stop focusing on the *'why?'* Everything we face in this life has a purpose, even if we don't understand it and it's hard to accept." Mark wrestled with the right words.

He opened the Bible in front of him to the book of Job and slid it across Ethan's kitchen island for him to see. "You've been reading Job, correct?" Ethan quietly nodded.

His silence allowed Mark to continue with his thought. "What did Job do when God allowed Satan to destroy his family?" It was a question Mark wanted Ethan to answer for himself, not to make him feel guilty, but to get the right idea into his head.

"He continued to praise God." Ethan's voice was barely audible as he tried to understand.

"When Job lost all his animals, what did he do?"

"He gave God praise."

Mark nodded and pressed his palms into the corners of the island. "Ethan, you were being held in the arms of a God who cared so much about you. He had a plan for your situation.

"I know your past was very sticky, but don't you see how God took the situation of your birth father and turned it into something beautiful when Nathaniel entered your life? Did you not trust that God could have done something just as miraculous when you lost your mom and stepdad in that car accident?" Mark needed to get his point across instead of speaking words in circles.

Thankfully, Ethan seemed intent on what Mark had to say.

"Our attitudes color our whole personality. We can't always choose what happens to us, but we *can* choose our attitudes toward each situation. And look, I have no idea how hard it must have been to lose people so close in your life. My two parents mean the world to me. *Hard* probably doesn't even begin to scratch the surface of describing what you went through. God gave you a big mountain to climb, but He knew you could have handled it. Instead of focusing on your problems and drowning your sorrows in alcohol, you should have held on to God and focused on His promises."

Mark exhaled as Ethan still wouldn't respond, he just listened with what seemed to be all his heart. "I'm not here to beat you up, Ethan, or tell you how awful you are. I'm here to help you defeat Satan's lies because you are more than his deceit. God can fill your holes of loneliness and emptiness." Mark knew in his heart that he was no longer talking to a drunk. He was talking to a friend who was capable of so much more.

"The book of Job gives us hope that like Job, persevering through trials and testing and remaining faithful to God, we are rewarded by Him. We come out battered and bruised, but also with newfound faith in God. How we act to our situations is crucial. We must not conclude that God has abandoned us, because he certainly didn't leave Job. Consistent faith is the way to defeat Satan."

Ethan ran his fingers through his hair and hopped off the barstool at the kitchen island. Seeming to need something to do, he grabbed two water bottles from his fridge. He opened one and handed the other to Mark.

Mark nodded as a thank you. "I don't want you to trust in God because my family, your sister, and I want you to. I want you to trust in God again, because *you* have the sincere and humble desire to. I do encourage you to read more in the Bible though. God promises a lot to those who believe in Him." Mark ended his session on that note, ready to see what step Ethan would make now.

He watched as Ethan closed his Bible shut. The man was noticeably getting more tired as wrinkles formed around his brows and dark bags developed under his eyes.

Mark longed for his friend to have a sense of peace only God could bring.

"I can't change my past…but I can change my future." Mark watched as Ethan trailed off from his words and seconds passed. "My mom used to tell me that." Ethan's half-smile assured Mark that he indeed received something out of today's counseling session.

"I'm sure she was a wise woman, as was your stepdad."

"They were." Ethan paused and shifted in his seat. "What time is church Sunday?"

"Ten in the morning." Mark couldn't hide his smile, for Ethan was asking the question without anyone inviting him first. It was a big step that Mark didn't figure Ethan would take for a few more weeks, but God's timing undoubtedly worked best.

A determined look surfaced his face as Ethan responded. "I'll try my very best to be there."

Mark nodded with a grateful grin as his cell phone rang. He read the caller ID and answered. "Hello, my little lobster." The epithet brought a smirk not only to Mark's face, but to Ethan's as well, for Ethan had caught on to Hope's family nickname.

A sickly version of Hope's voice sounded over the phone, and she didn't even acknowledge his remark about her nickname. "Mark, I have the flu." She groaned.

"Are you alright?" Ethan perked up like a dog would at the word *treat* at Mark's question.

"I would be okay if I wasn't sick." She laid the sarcasm on thick. "Look, I was just wondering if you could stop by and drop off some soup from that diner downtown by the fire department."

Mark glanced at his watch. "You're lucky I have thirty minutes before my meeting with the mayor."

"Bless you." She sneezed just before he hung up the phone.

"No, bless you." He hooted at his corny joke.

"Leave the jokes to me." She managed a weak chuckle. "Thank you."

"No problem." Mark hung up his phone.

"What's wrong with Hope?" Ethan asked as soon as Mark shoved his cell phone in his back pocket.

Mark laughed at Ethan's enthusiasm. "Easy, tiger. Hope's alright." Mark reassured him. "You're becoming quite interested in my little sister, aren't you?" He grabbed his heavy winter coat. "She has the flu," Mark explained.

Ethan nodded, not denying Mark's rhetorical question. "I should call and check on her later."

"She would enjoy that. I'm supposed to stop by the diner and pick up her favorite soup." Mark headed toward the door as Ethan trailed behind him. "Used and abused, I am," he teased.

Mark turned around at the door to see Ethan inwardly debating with himself. Ethan rubbed his bottom lip with his thumb. "I could go get it. I need an excuse to talk to her."

His offer was nice, but Mark didn't know whether Hope would appreciate the

213

company right now. "She gets grumpy when she's sick," he warned.

"I think I can handle her." Ethan winked.

Mark stopped before heading out into the frigid winter day. He felt it necessary to bring out Big Brother Bear. "Please treat her well. Hope's a princess and I don't want to see her heart break."

Ethan shoved his hands in his pocket. "She wants me to believe again." He rocked on his heels like a child would.

"We all do, but none of us want it to be guilt driven." Mark slipped his shoes on. "You don't have to have all your questions answered to make the first step. God will help you out with the rest. We're all here for you, Ethan…Hope especially. She enjoys spending her time with you. As her brother, I can tell she's genuinely happy when around you."

"I don't want to let her down." Ethan appeared heartbroken just at the thought, which made Mark feel good inside…being the big brother and all.

Mark sighed. "Take her the soup, Ethan. You mentioned church, so go to church with all of us Sunday. You might surprise yourself and find yourself enjoying it. Then, who knows? Maybe we'll go out to eat afterward."

"I will," Ethan agreed, seeming content with his decision.

"In the end though, it's not about her. It's about you and *your* heart," Mark added before he trudged off into the outdoors' grey winter wonderland.

Ethan walked into Funfetti Café and Bakery, letting the door jingle behind him. For a mid-Monday morning, the line wasn't too bad.

So far, he purchased Hope a funny get-well card, a fluffy teddy bear, a dozen multi-colored roses, and her favorite soup from Patti's Diner. His mission now was to find out her favorite dessert. Hope had done so much for him, so it was time that he paid her back. Not that he had to, but his heart desired to.

215

"Hi there, Ethan! What can I get for you today?" Cheery Anne met him on the other side of the counter as he stepped up for his turn to order.

"Hi, Anne." Ethan grinned. The thirty some year-old woman's bubbliness reminded him of his mom. "I was wondering if Brianna might be around here somewhere. I have a question for her."

"She's around here somewhere. I'll go hunt her down for 'ya." She shot him a smile before heading through the kitchen door.

Ethan took this time to survey all the desserts behind the glass counter. One could clearly perceive Hope and Brianna's passion exhibited on the shelves upon shelves of desserts—Tie-dye cookies, homemade donuts, gourmet muffins, and so many gorgeously decorated cakes with intricate details. This bakery was where Hope's heart was.

Hope's love for her job made Ethan's heart ache. He missed what he used to do. Coaching the high school soccer team was something he enjoyed immensely, along with the simple day job he'd once possessed in an office. Being around kids and teaching them skills in something he was passionate about—it was what he looked forward to most. The thought of considering job hunting dwelled on Ethan's mind lately. He suddenly missed putting effort into something and feeling accomplished at the end of the day.

He pushed aside his thoughts as Hope's younger sister appeared from the kitchen. "You're covered in flour." Ethan's lips curved into a smirk at her appearance. Brianna's apron was smothered in chocolate frosting, and her platinum blonde hair seemed even whiter with a coat of powdered sugar and flour.

Brianna laughed. "Thanks for reminding me. A bag ripped, and I happened to be carrying it." She dusted her hands off on her jeans. "This bakery doesn't fully function without Hope, but don't tell her I said that."

He chuckled. "Speaking of Hope, I was wondering if you knew what her favorite dessert was." He leaned against the counter, awaiting Brianna's reply.

Bri formed a cunning grin. "As long as I can make the speech at your guys' wedding."

217

Ethan was positive his eyes grew larger than a fifty-cent coin at Brianna's statement. "You're ridiculous, you know that?" He laughed. "She's sick and I'm just going to check in on her," he explained, knowing he didn't have to clarify himself, but he felt the need to.

"Mhmm." She raised her eyebrows then giggled like a little schoolgirl. "She likes strawberry shortcakes...not too much whipped topping, and strawberries are her favorite fruit."

Ethan nodded as he noted the information about Hope.

Hope's sister continued. "Lucky for you, I have two extra cakes that were freshly made a about thirty minutes ago. The woman who originally ordered them canceled. I was going to put them behind the counter, but they're all yours," she offered.

"Sweet." Ethan snagged the offer. "How much do I owe you?"

She shook her head as she grabbed two bakery boxes under the counter. "Make my sister happy and it's free. I'll call and find out how her evening went, you know. If she didn't enjoy it, then you owe me," Bri taunted.

Ethan found himself liking Hope's little sister more and more. She had a charming sense of humor but deep-down, Brianna cared vastly for her family. He admired that. "Thank you." He smiled as she headed to the back to box the two cakes.

The knocking at Hope's apartment door pounded in her head. She sat up from her couch, and dizziness met her as she stood. She wrapped a plush pink blanket around her body and headed for the door. Like a snail, her body trailed slowly along the path to the front door. Her tangled hair, odd colored skin, and glasses were going to make her brother run.

She opened the door. "It's about ti—" she stopped in her tracks when she realized it wasn't her brother standing at her door.

Instead, Ethan Grey stood patiently waiting on her apartment door mat. Bundled in a heavy Carhartt coat, he shivered. Ethan blew a strand of hair out of his face, still dusted with specks of snow as inches of white flakes piled up outside. Clutched in his right arm was a teddy bear with a smiley face balloon and card in its paw. Hope eyed vibrant roses in Ethan's large grip as well. His left hand held a bag that smelled of her favorite soup.

Hope suddenly realized she looked a mess compared to the handsome man standing in front of her. Her cheeks heated and she pushed her hair behind her ears in attempt to make herself look better. She didn't want Ethan to see her this way, but she had no other choice right now. "Come in, you've got chills." She stepped aside to let him in.

He stepped into her apartment and took off his boots. "It's snowing hard." She watched as he shrugged his coat off. His grey sweater showed off his muscles in all the right places. She'd decided a long time ago that he looked handsome in just about anything. Hope ripped her gaze from his biceps as Ethan began to speak. "I hope you don't mind. I happened to be there when you rang Mark. I may or may not have intruded."

Hope didn't realize how much she missed his warm smile until now. "I don't mind at all. I enjoy surprises." She grinned. "Although, I look like a train just ran me over."

He stopped in his tracks. "You look beautiful…as always." The admiration in the twinkle of his chestnut eyes was too much for her to handle.

"You're too kind. I've seen myself in the mirror today." Hope walked him into her cozy living space.

He chuckled. "These are all yours." He handed over the teddy bear holding the balloon and card, along with the multi-colored roses. "Think of it as an apology gift too. I messed up." He offered a remorseful smile.

"We all mess up." She traced a finger over a delicate rose petal. "They're beautiful." She looked up at him with a smile.

Ethan's relief was evident as the tension from his shoulders released and he began to relax. "Lead me to your kitchen, and then go lie back down. I come bearing lots of food."

"Good, I'm starved." Her stomach had been roaring ever since she had thrown up the last of its contents.

She strolled into her small kitchen, Ethan on her heels. "The bowls are in—" Hope started to show Ethan where all her utensils were when he gently placed his hand on her shoulder.

"I can handle this, go lie down." The touch was electric, and suddenly Hope was thankful she could go sit down.

She stifled a laugh and walked back to her living room space, the warm fireplace calling her. She placed the bear and roses Ethan had gotten her on the small mantle above the fireplace. Hope glanced out by the window overlooking the quiet, snowy city of Alton as she opened the card the bear had been holding. She found herself laughing out loud at the cheesy joke on the inside.

"I'm guessing you read the card?" The corners of Ethan's lips lifted, and dimples appeared on his cheeks as he appeared from the kitchen with two soup mugs full of steaming homemade chicken noodles.

She nodded and bit her bottom lip. "It was a good one." She laughed once more and placed the card with the rest of her gifts.

He nodded toward the couch and Hope shuffled her feet behind him. Ethan let her take her seat and get comfortable first before handing her the warm soup. Patti's chicken noodle soup always made her mouth ooze at the delicious smelling aroma.

"How are you feeling?" He sat down at the opposite corner of the couch.

"If I'm being completely honest…awful." She groaned at the uncontrollable shivers that snaked their way down her body.

Ethan grabbed an extra blanket at the foot of the couch and wrapped it around her with the blanket that had already been by her side. "Have you been to the doctor?"

"I did after Bri shooed me away from work. It's the flu. They prescribed an antibiotic, but so far it's not a miracle worker." She muted her TV from the movie she had been watching earlier. "I'd hate for you to get it." Hope grimaced at the thought of making him miserable.

"I get to see you, so it's worth the risk." He grinned.

She shook her head with a laugh. "This soup is fantastic."

He agreed and pointed out her tree in the corner of the living room. "Your Christmas tree isn't *that* bad." Trying to cover up his awful lie, Ethan slurped his soup, almost choking on it as he did so.

Her tree was somewhere under the thick, multi-colored tinsel. Every time Hope glanced in its direction, she wanted to bury her face in her decorative pillows. Brianna definitely over-did it with the decorations this year. "You're very bad at lying." She chuckled and wrinkled her nose. "But thanks for trying to make me feel better."

Ethan threw his head back as he laughed. The sound was better medicine than the anti-biotics the doctor prescribed Hope.

"Speaking of Christmas—once I get to feeling better, I still have some last-minute gifts to purchase." Hope wanted to buy her sister something for her kitchen, and she wanted to get the church youth class something special.

"Give me a day, and I'll tag along and get us lunch. Plus, I'm not good at shopping for Sara." The flicker of fear in his wide eyes made Hope snort.

"That would be fun." She grinned, then added, "And we ladies love anything that smells good and sparkles." Hope quoted words from her mother's mouth.

"It's harder than that."

"I think you're being dramatic, but nonetheless, I'll help you out." Hope reassured him with a wink. "How is Sara?" Hope hadn't seen Ethan's sister since they went black Friday shopping. She missed her friend.

"Good. She's back to work now and staying busy with crazy round the clock shifts again. She cares a whole lot about her patients. Sara's good at what she does." Hope smiled at how Ethan talked about his sister. One could tell the two of them were trying to bond now as siblings should.

Hope's stomach abruptly began to churn, protesting the food she'd been hungrily devouring. She placed her hand over her belly to try to make it stop. *Not now,*

225

Lord. Please, not right now. "Good." She placed her half empty soup mug on the coffee table.

"Are you alright?" Ethan asked, probably catching the wince she tried her best to hide.

"No." She couldn't cover the pain up. Her body shook uncontrollably, and her woozy head made the living space spin. She could almost taste the bile rising in her throat for the fourth time today.

"What do you need me to do?" He urgently sat his empty bowl on the side table and knelt in front of her.

Hope motioned him up toward her. "Come here." With a puzzled look, he obeyed without questioning her request by sitting directly beside her on the couch.

She took a pillow and laid it in his lap, then curled into a ball to rest her head on the pillow. Ethan pulled the blankets further up her body as she clutched her stomach. The flu was absolute torture. She looked up to see Ethan's soft smile full of sympathy. "I don't like being sick," Hope groaned.

226

"I don't think anyone does." He pushed her long bangs out of her face with small strokes of his finger. "If you feel up to it later, I brought dessert. Fresh strawberry shortcake." He offered her a half-smile.

She was falling in love with the dimpled smile that made Ethan's eyes crinkle around the edges. Hope felt herself on the brink of tears, for Ethan had made her day a lot brighter, and a bit more bearable. He'd brought her gifts, her favorite dessert and soup, but most importantly he'd given her his time. "Thank you," she whispered as her eyelids drew heavy.

Ethan gently leaned down to kiss her forehead as a reply. The gesture was enough to make her tingle all the way from her forehead to her toes. She couldn't fight the sleep as he began to trace the brown spotted freckles on her cheeks with his pointer finger. With each tender stroke, Hope's heart caught itself falling in love with Ethan Grey.

Ethan stepped into his home later that night. He hadn't wanted to leave Hope alone in her condition, but luckily Hope's parents were on their way to check on her when he left.

His heart ached as he reflected on holding her hand and her hair back as she threw up her dinner on the bathroom floor. The flu was beating her to a pulp. He didn't like seeing Hope—normally so strong— weak.

Slipping his shoes off, Ethan headed up the stairs of his quiet house to his bedroom. He needed a shower, some sleep, and then he would check on Hope first thing in the morning. Seeing her so sick strangely made him want to always be there...through her worst times and her best times. It was a desire that developed over time in his heart. Hope meant a lot to him and his frail heart.

As he entered his bedroom, his landline phone rang from the nightstand by his bed. He jogged over to answer it, hoping that if it was Hope, she was okay.

"Hello?" He plopped down on the edge of his bed.

A voice spoke on the other end faster than the blizzard coming down outside. "I just got off the phone with Hope. She had a wonderful time and appreciated your visit. So, the cake is free." Ethan recognized the voice as none other than Hope's little sister, Brianna.

He erupted in laughter, enjoying more and more the company of the Lawson family. When he caught his breath, he replied, "I didn't know you were serious."

"And what makes you think I'd lie?" She asked, her matter-of-fact tone crystal clear.

Ethan laughed and shook his head. If he had a future with Hope, keeping up with a close-knit family would be one thing...keeping up with Brianna would be another. He found the thought both amusing and intriguing.

thirteen

"I hate to tell you, but Santa Claus isn't real."

She shoved the salted caramel popcorn in his face. "Could you hush for like five seconds?" They'd been watching *The Santa Clause* with Tim Allen, one of Hope's favorites. Ethan may like binging movies, but he sure didn't know how to keep quiet during them.

He laid his head back on the couch and laughed. "I'm keeping you entertained."

He popped the popcorn she'd thrown at him in his mouth.

"Isn't that what the movie is for?" Hope teased as Ethan stuck his tongue out at her.

Ethan had come over to check on Hope's health the next day. He'd brought old Christmas movies, hot chocolate to keep her warm, and all kinds of salty foods. For that, Hope was feeling better in spirits. The sickness settled in to stay for a while, so she figured she'd make the best of the situation for now.

Hope smiled to herself as she wriggled under a blanket. She'd never enjoyed someone's company this much until now. Ethan proved how much Hope meant to him just in the past couple of days through his kind gestures. It wasn't like she'd been making him stay or begging him to come back to her. He simply was there for her, and it beat being alone and sick to a pulp. She was coming to love having him by her side, for she felt safe there.

"Feeling better?" he asked, gently tilting his head to rest on her shoulder.

"I'm doing pretty well at the moment." Hope kept her eyes on the movie. This was her favorite time of the year. Lying by the fire, watching Christmas films, and baking. Oh, how she missed baking already. "Although, I am missing work." She sighed and turned her head to glance at Ethan.

His eyes were rarely glazed over with a dark, glassy film of depression anymore. In fact, the corners of his eyes were beginning to leave lines where he smiled so much recently. His normal combed-back, and perfectly fixed hair was more undone today. It caused a smile to tug at Hope's lips.

"I know." Ethan simply stated. He caressed his fingers through her hair and hummed along with a Christmas tune that played in the background of the film.

"You're happy." Hope pulled the heavy blanket up to her chin.

"I am." He grinned at her.

Feeling him divide her straight hair into three different sections, Hope bit her lip to stifle a giggle. "Are you braiding my hair?"

"I'm trying…but failing." He snickered and continued to play with her tangled hair.

"I'll give you an *A* for effort." She chuckled and found herself leaning into his arms. She wanted another nap, and he just so happened to be a wonderful leaning post.

With Ethan stroking her hair and holding her so dearly, Hope nearly closed her eyes to sleep. She felt content in his arms, like nothing could ever go wrong. Although, knowing the truth was far more complicated than that, she let out a sigh. Hope wanted to freeze this moment in time because she figured Ethan and her wouldn't go on like this forever.

"Ethan, why did you always come to Funfetti?" The question was one that dwelled on her mind recently. Hope loved her café and bakery, but never thought it entertaining enough to be there every single morning.

He shifted his position on the couch and exhaled. "I was so used to having breakfast with my parents and sister in the morning. It was something we just always did. Change is weird, and it's the little things

233

that are so hard to adjust to. That was one of them.

"So, on one of my awful, hungover mornings, I stumbled upon a warm little bakery. This pretty girl with strawberry-blonde hair and just enough freckles welcomed me in. She provided me with breakfast and coffee on the house. Made me feel special and wanted." Ethan playfully smiled as he described Hope. "Your place felt inviting. Everyone was warm and friendly, and I enjoyed being there. In so much heartbreak, I felt a bit at peace."

Hope choked back tears that willed their way to her eyes. She didn't know the deeper meaning behind Ethan being at her bakery so often. It warmed her heart that something like a simple bakery could have such an impact in someone's life. Tucking that fact away in a pocket of her heart, Hope thanked God for His bigger plans.

"It may sound cheesy, but you made my mornings brighter. Your kindness affected me, even if it didn't show on the outside." He rubbed her shoulders. "You still do, by the way," Ethan added.

Hope grinned. Ethan was making his way into her heart. "I'm glad."

They both settled back onto the couch, watching the movie. Hope could easily get used to him being by her side. She enjoyed being with her family and friends, but Ethan was different. His gentle, caring personality overruled his ugly past. It was the miniscule things he did for her that brought a smile to her lips. The way he was overcoming obstacles and incorporating her in it all as he went. And the fact that he was still taking care of her while she looked and felt a mess.

But there was still a gap between him and her…a deep, huge gap. Her heart constricted at the thought. He didn't have her God in his life. He was beating the alcohol and depression slowly, but he didn't have the peace from his past that the Holy Spirit brought, like she did.

Having distinctly different beliefs would chew them up and spit them out if they ever decided to be anything more than friends. She couldn't live her life like that, but if Ethan turned to God…

Hope shook her head at such selfish thoughts. She couldn't make him believe for her benefit. Ethan had to make the decision himself.

God, I'm normally more optimistic than this. Forgive me for my selfishness. I've been asking for Ethan to give his heart to You. Part of that is because I've been wanting it to benefit me in hopes of a relationship with him. But I no longer want to pray for it to benefit me. *His soul is so precious, Lord. He needs a Savior more than an earthly relationship. You can give him so much more than I can, help him realize that. I now desire for him to seek You more than I desire a relationship with him. Help me to lead him to You. I'm giving this one to You.*

The movie flicked to a commercial break and Hope positioned herself at an angle where she wouldn't get light-headed. "Ask me a question, any kind of question. Commercial breaks are boring. So, *this* is where you can keep me entertained." Hope could tell her request surprised Ethan, but she watched as he thought about it.

"What would your ideal date night be like if someone were to ask you out in the winter time?"

Hope quirked an eyebrow. Ethan was taking advantage of her request. Nonetheless, she would answer just to satisfy him. "I would say bowling, ice cream for the winner after, because I'm quite a pro if I must say so myself." Ethan laughed at the way she bragged. "Then, looking at Christmas lights and listening to Holiday music."

"You haven't thought about this much, have you?" He poked fun at her.

"A girl can dream."

Ethan's eyebrows furrowed as his facial expression turned more pensive. "Why don't I make that small dream come true then?"

"I think I would say yes." She answered with a grin.

Ethan wore a satisfied smile. "What about after church this Sunday?"

Taken aback, her heart thumped so loudly in her chest that she was fearful Ethan would hear it. "You want to go to church?"

"I think I do." He nervously chewed on his bottom lip.

237

She couldn't control her goofy looking grin. "Let's hope I get better by this weekend."

"I hope so too. Mark mentioned something about getting lunch after with all of us."

"I would enjoy that." Hope smiled and pulled her legs up to her chin as chills rushed down her back. "My brother is always up to something." She laughed.

Ethan cocked his head to the side, not understanding. "What do you mean?" Noticing her shivers, he took the blanket she'd been using and tucked her in snuggly.

"He once set me up with his partner, Brandon. Mark went on a date and he didn't want to go alone. So, he asked me to go on a double date with Brandon. Like the couple of other guys in my past, it didn't work out. Brandon was sweet, but we just weren't right for each other." Hope paused. "Plus, he has a *thing* for my sister, always has." She grinned as she thought about Brandon's love for her little sister.

"Is it okay if I do tag along for church and lunch, then you and I go out to look at lights after?" he asked sincerely, checking with her.

"Of course. Long as you don't make me walk back. Jonathan was also a mistake." She sighed, knowing she'd never had the best of experiences with guys.

"What kind of guys did you date?" His horrified expression made Hope snort.

"Not very bright ones...that's for sure." Hope stood and situated herself in front of the fireplace. The freezing chills were uncontrollable. "What about you? Any smart, blonde bakers?" She managed to wiggle her eyebrows without her belly rumbling the wrong way.

Ethan doubled over in laughter. "No. One brunette in eleventh grade, though. My mom was the sweetest person on earth and she wasn't even fond of her. The girl wanted me to change and drop everything for her, especially soccer. That's when I said sayonara, sister."

Hope snickered. "I recall high school drama."

"Then a blonde after I graduated." He twiddled his thumbs. "We were actually

239

serious. She got a job offer in New York to be a magazine reporter and took it. I didn't want to leave Alton, it was home. So, we ended the relationship before it got complicated and ugly," he admitted; his soft brown eyes glued on Hope.

"I'm sorry, Ethan."

"I'm not. If it wasn't meant to be, it wasn't meant to be. You know?" He took a sip of his coffee sitting on the end table.

"I understand completely." Hope nodded, liking the way he thought.

Christmas music started to chime on Hope's TV again and Ethan cleared his throat, "Come on." He patted the seat next to him. "The movie's back on, and you need to get warm."

fourteen

Hope laughed to herself as she hung up the phone and placed it on her bedside table. Ethan would appreciate the knock-knock joke and thank you on his answering machine once he got home.

Her Tuesday evening with him had been nice, even if her health hadn't been up to par. After she took a nap, Ethan had ordered a Chicago style deep dish pizza and offered to play a game of Scrabble with her. Hope let him win. She blamed it on being sick, but it was an excuse just to see his smile. She found herself envisioning many more evenings spent like tonight in the future. It was the small things that meant a lot.

She rolled back the duvet cover on her bed and snuggled underneath of it. Trying to find a comfortable position between constant shivers and a grumbling stomach was complicated but she eventually drifted off to sleep.

"Ethan, don't do this." Hope's sobs were uncontrollable. Tremors rippled through her body as she watched the man she loved down another bottle of alcohol.

Where was Mark? He was supposed to be here with help by now.

"Why not?" Ethan gripped the glass bottle so tight that his knuckles turned white. He staggered all over his house, pacing. Hope lost count of how many bottles he'd downed since he called her. "I've lost everything."

"Because there is *hope. You don't have to do this." She flinched as he threw the bottle toward the corner of his kitchen. Glass shattered into a million tiny fragments.*

"And you don't have to follow me around like I'm some child! My decision has already been made." He hovered over Hope's body and she suddenly felt so small. What was left of her heart, broke as she watched the man who made so much progress, easily fall back into his old ways. She almost regretted getting to know Ethan, but she knew he was more than the bottles of poison and she thought he recognized that too.

"You're going to regret your decision one day." Hope's voice cracked.

Ethan stumbled, but he managed to walk briskly out the kitchen and toward his front door. Tears streamed down her face as Hope watched him grab his keys. *"It was nice knowing you, Hope."*

Hope's knees gave out and she teetered on her heels. *"I beg of you, Ethan, don't do this!"*

He opened the door and his glassy eyes met hers. "Too late."

Mark Lawson's POV

The incessant whooping of Mark's police car siren drummed to the rhythm of his heart. He was going eighty on frozen roads, but it didn't matter at this moment. Ethan was going to attempt suicide, Mark was sure of it.

"Brandon, call for backup," Mark instructed his tense partner sitting in the passenger seat.

Brandon immediately obeyed without asking questions.

Snow fell rapidly from the skies, making his vision even cloudier. The adrenaline rush made Mark's hands shake as he drove. If Hope was at Ethan's house...

He shook the thought from his head, not needing to involve his emotions in this mission yet.

God, please keep my sister safe. Don't let any lives be taken. Stop Ethan somehow. My heart is beating out of my chest and all I can say is, "God, please."

Mark knew his prayer wouldn't go unheard, even if it did seem like the plea was jumbled. God would answer in the best way possible, because He understood.

"Mark, I see headlights," Brandon shouted over the engine and siren.

The white snow illuminated Ethan's all too familiar red truck. Rolled down a bank so close to the Mississippi river, was Ethan's overturned truck. Mark's police car skidded on the road as he pressed firmly on the brakes. He safely pulled to the side of the road and turned on his emergency flashers. To help him see down the bank better, Mark switched his lights to high beam and sprinted through the snow to the overturned truck.

"The truck has flipped!" Mark shouted to Brandon.

When he'd made it to the bottom of the slushy bank, he crawled on all fours through the wet snow toward the shattered window of the driver's side. "Ethan, can you hear me?" Mark couldn't let his friend, who'd fallen into relapse, die. It couldn't happen.

Mark frantically grabbed his flashlight from his belt and switched it on. Squinting his eyes to adjust to the harsh light, he expelled all breath at the sight of blood splattered all over the inside of the truck. When he spotted Ethan's lifeless body,

245

Mark's shoulders slumped, and tears threatened to spill from his burning eyes.

"God, help us."

Hope jerked upright from her bed. The quick motion made her head spin, tempting the pizza from earlier to come back up. Sweat poured from her brow and she wiped at it with the back of her hand. She took a shaky breath, trying to get a grip on what she just vividly dreamed. "God." Her heart skipped a beat. "Please save Ethan." Her unsteady breath worried her, but not as much as Ethan's Salvation.

She moved to the right of her bed and flicked the lamp on, wincing at the sudden bright light. Hope took one glance at her clock that read 3:00 A.M. and grabbed her phone. The time didn't matter at this moment. She needed to hear Ethan's voice. She needed him to feel God like she felt God. His soul was too precious.

After a few rings, Ethan's groggy and raspy voice answered. "Hope? Is everything alright? It's three in the morning."

Just the sound of his well-alive voice helped her breathe a little better. "I don't want to be separated an eternity from you, Ethan." She let the salty tears cascade down her face. Hope didn't want her friend to die without God. Eternity was long spent in torment and darkness.

Ethan didn't reply for what felt like forever to Hope. Maybe he was trying to wake up, or maybe he was trying to sink in what she abruptly called him for. "Neither do I." He tried to diminish the crack in his voice by clearing his throat. Ethan knew exactly what Hope was talking about.

"Then please, Ethan, please take care of your heart and soul. Not because I want you to, but because I care too much for you to not care about where you stand with God." Shivers ran up Hope's spine. She was getting more nauseous by the minute.

"I want to be at church Sunday." His simple statement made the crazy fluttering of Hope's heart settle. "Are you okay?" His worried voice reflected her own.

"Yes." Hope laid back down and pulled the bed covers up to her shoulders.

247

FINDING HOPE

For the next hour, she listened to Ethan's soothing voice as he talked to her about random things, probably trying to calm her worries. The sound of his strong voice was enough to make her nightmare slowly fade away. While he took the time to make small talk with her, Hope prayed without ceasing for Ethan's broken soul.

Friday morning, Ethan stepped out of his truck into the frigid winter weather. The gloves he wore on his hands weren't helping whatsoever with the numbness he felt deep inside. He walked to the passenger side of his truck and helped Sara out. Having his sister here with him on this occasion felt right.

Today would have marked their stepdad and mom's sixteenth anniversary of being married, and Sara and Ethan both wanted to honor them. It didn't feel that long ago when Ethan walked his mom down the aisle to marry Nathaniel. The memories didn't seem that far away to him, yet in reality, he knew they were millions of miles away.

The morning was a beautiful one, besides the cold temperature. The graveyard was private, on top of a hill in a secluded area. The sunrise of colors glistened on the fresh layer of snow blanketed atop the grass. His mom would have loved today's magenta and crimson sunrise. And Nathaniel would have loved to start a snowball fight with the dense snow on the ground.

While he didn't want to, Ethan let his mind settle on his birth father, Peter. The scars of Peter and how he treated Ethan's family were still there, but they weren't as raw and emotional as before. Ethan felt his insides beginning to heal and let things go, for he had his own story to tell and he didn't want to repeat the poor choices Peter made in the past.

Ethan glanced to his right at his older sister as they walked up the small cemented staircase that led to gravesites. She wore a solemn look on her face. Sara was a splitting image of their mom, Kate, and held the one characteristic that Kate always was: strong. She let her emotions and thoughts build up on the inside until she felt the need to speak her mind. It built her character, though. It made

249

her tough. It made her someone to love so carefully.

"Mom would be proud of you, Sara." Ethan clutched his big sister's left hand.

Sara let a single tear trickle down her cheek as she squeezed Ethan's hand. In her other hand, she held on tight to two bouquets of red roses.

They slowly approached their mom and Nathaniel's grave. It'd been forever since Ethan visited. The site always made him rage with anger and sent him into depression. Today, though? He strangely felt at peace.

"They're in a much better place." Sara placed a bouquet of roses on both of their parent's headstones.

Ethan let a tear fall from his own face as his jaw locked. Emotions were easier to express rather than hold back for him. There was no use for him to bottle it all up. Thoughts circled in his head.

Is it just the bones of my parents below me? Are their souls really in the unimaginable Heaven?

He wanted to believe it. He wanted so badly to believe that he would see his parents again one day.

After Hope explained her phone call to him Tuesday night, it had put Ethan on edge ever since. If it were all real, there were two places to spend his eternity. Ethan wanted to go to Heaven. He never wanted to hurt anyone or most importantly, leave life unprepared. The thought petrified him and quickened his pulse.

Why didn't I have the faith I once possessed as a kid?

Ethan embraced Sara into a warm hug when he saw her shiver. If it wasn't for her, he might be far worse than he was in this moment. Learning to cherish his sister hadn't been that hard when reality hit him in the face. She was all he had left of his parents, and he would choose to love that connection with his entire heart.

She stood there in his hold during a string of silence. "Is that drawing on the wall still in Nathaniel's office?" Sara asked, trying to lighten Ethan's mood.

251

"Still there." Ethan chuckled at the memory. At age ten, Ethan became jealous of Sara for getting all the attention after breaking her arm on the trampoline. In attempt to steal some of her glory, he'd snuck into his stepdad's office with a permanent marker to doodle. It got everyone's attention...that was for sure.

"Nathaniel never did want to paint over it." Sara shoved her hands in her coat pockets.

"He secretly loved it," Ethan added, making Sara laugh.

Sara's smile slowly faded as she looked back down at the two graves, a symbolization of two beautiful lives. "Our parents are gone, Ethan." Like a wave, shock hit Sara once more.

Ethan tried to stand strong for his sister by placing his hand on her shoulder. "Hey, we're going to get through this, okay? One day at a time. Together. No more doing this alone anymore." He wiped a wet tear from her eye with his thumb. She slowly nodded and buried her head in his chest.

Instantly, he felt like he was rolling back to the time that he never originally gave Sara. It was time to grow up and be a man. To shoulder some of her pain and take this chance to be there for his sister. From now on, he would be the brother that cared for his sister's thoughts and emotions.

"I'm sorry, Sara." Ethan whispered into her shoulder. He couldn't come up with enough of apologies. He'd never been there for her. For three years, Sara had been on her own because Ethan was too selfish to think about anyone else's feelings but his. He owed his sister so much.

Sara pulled back to look at him and her blue eyes misted. "There is no need for apologies, Ethan."

"You are wrong. There are many reasons I should apologize and because those reasons are countless, just know that I am sincerely sorry...for everything."

Sara sighed and let a small, half-smile form. "I know." She gripped his hand once more and leaned on his side. "Let's go bro, I need to get ready for work."

Ethan nodded, took one last look at his parent's headstones, and hesitantly walked Sara back to his truck. "Let's do a dinner on Christmas Eve. Me, you, Hope, Mark, and Brianna. We'll even do a gift swap."

"As long as I can buy the gag gift." A sly smile formed on Sara's face, making Ethan thankful that her grim expression was beginning to lighten up.

He laughed with a nod that gave her permission. "I'll call them and set it up."

fifteen

Ethan pulled his truck in Hope's driveway Sunday morning. Snow blanketed the ground, but the sun was out, and blue skies brightened the morning even greater. The birds chirped to an unknown melody, and to Ethan, something seemed fresh about the scenery around him. It was going to be a beautiful day; he could sense it.

Friday afternoon consisted of looking for jobs but failing to find one of his interest. That evening Hope surprised him by bringing over a homemade casserole for dinner. The sweet gesture reassured him that Hope genuinely cared for his wellbeing.

Now on the mend from her case of the flu, Ethan was happy to see her spirits liven back up. While he enjoyed her company and friendship, he wasn't going to lie...he loved the food too.

Saturday, Ethan convinced her to go ice skating with him. Since skates were shoes that he hadn't known how to navigate, he'd felt like a deer first learning how to walk. Thankfully, Hope helped him navigate and get on his feet, even if she did laugh at him every now and then. After they skated, he took her back to his place to get warmed up. They watched a Christmas film and he made her his mother's homemade hot chocolate recipe. The perfect way to end a wonderful weekend.

He took another look at himself in his visor mirror before pulling the key from the ignition and hopping out of his truck. He wore simple blue jeans and a maroon sweater, not wanting to overdress, but he still put forth effort. He also spent way more time on his hair this morning than he was willing to admit.

His clammy hands shook as he approached the apartment complex and took the stairs to Hope's door. He didn't believe his nervousness stemmed from being in Hope's presence. It was the fact that he would be stepping foot into a church again. Not just for counseling, but to attend an actual service.

It's not too late to go back home.

With his feet planted in front of Hope's apartment door, Ethan shook his head at his thought. He *wanted* to go. His heart felt a small tug toward church and that in itself felt enough for him this morning.

Ethan's knuckles were knocking on the door before he could be a coward and back out. He heard Hope holler from behind the door and seconds later she swung the heavy brown door open. Struggling to strap her black heel on her left foot, she almost toppled over him with the whoosh of the door.

Ethan reached his hands out to steady her as she finished slipping her shoes on. His eyes met her glistening ones as she softly smiled. He studied what she was wearing: an emerald knee length, long sleeved velvet dress that complimented her eyes and figure. Her black heels made her just a bit taller, but Ethan's height still towered over her. Curled

257

today, a section of her hair was pulled back with a shiny silver barrette.

He went back to studying her gorgeous face. She didn't wear her makeup too heavy, and Ethan appreciated that because he loved seeing her freckles in full bloom. She looked stunning.

Ethan motioned for her to spin around, and she twirled with a giggle. Once she finished her 360, she stopped to look at him. "Hi."

Her cheeky smile made Ethan grin.

"Good morning, pretty thing."

Hope shifted her weight from side to side. "Let me grab my coat and Bible, and I'll be ready." Ethan loved the fact that he could make her cheeks turn red so easily.

He nodded as Hope disappeared in her house to gather her belongings. A few minutes later, she met him back at the door. With her keys, she locked the door.

"Ready?" He asked as his heartbeat skyrocketed at the question that felt directed more to himself than Hope.

She nodded with a simple smile and locked her left arm with his right one as he led her out the complex to his truck. "Let's go to church."

The choir sang effortlessly in angelic voices to Hope's favorite song. "Your Cries Have Awoken the Master." Goosebumps chilled their way up and down Hope's arms and she pulled her cardigan wrap closer around her. The song rang true to the season of life she was in. Each little lyric spoke to her in numerous ways.

Hope had been praying every single night for Ethan's relationship with God to be restored. She was clinging to God for this situation, for He was the only hope that was possible. God was hearing her desperate prayer. Hope had no doubt of it. He recognized Hope's voice, because she was His child. This battle was almost over. God was going to bring something well out of this situation, because she cried out to Him. She could tell by the Holy Ghost bumps on her arms and by how Ethan had a desire to come with her this morning that *something* was going to happen.

Ethan's hands had been shaking when they entered the church fifteen minutes ago. Hope felt his fingers go cold as he sat down in their seat when they first arrived. The welcoming church that she attended made Ethan's nerves settle enough for him to know that they weren't going to jump down his throat for his wrong doings. That would be hypocritical.

Hope loved her church dearly and admired the strong body of believers of all ages. It was the church she had been raised in her entire life. With deep roots bound here, she had no plan or desire to leave. Alton was home.

Sara arrived late from a night shift of work and settled in the pew directly in front of Hope and Ethan. Hope's sister, Brianna sat to the left of Hope, her gaze settled on the choir. Her parents were here as well. Mark sat on the front pew where all the ministers sat, and his partner Brandon sat in the pew behind him. Hope truly believed she saw Brandon wink at Bri before service started. Those two were as blind as bats when it came to love.

A gentle nudge on her left shoulder took Hope back to reality. She turned to her sister who was handing her a Bible that was open to highlighted Scripture. Taking the Bible into her hands, Hope read Isaiah 40:31. She could barely see the verse through the tears that threatened their way out.

"But they that wait upon the LORD shall renew their *strength; they shall mount up with wings as eagles; they shall run, and not be weary;* and *they shall walk, and not faint."*

She gingerly handed the Bible back to Brianna. "Thank you," Hope whispered as she wiped her eyes. Her sister could read Hope like the back of her hand. Hope needed that reassurance. *Thank You, God.*

Her sister returned a satisfied smile and turned her attention back on the service.

Hope glanced to her left at Ethan, who seemed to be admiring the songs that the choir sang. God was going to bring something good of today. She *felt* it. She just had to wait on His perfect timing. Then her strength would be renewed, and she would soar.

Ethan felt as if the stifling hot air was suffocating him. Thirty minutes had passed since the choir sang their beautiful arrangements. Bible classes were now over, and kids were back in seats with their parents. Dressed in a nice suit, Mark confidently walked up the steps of the pulpit to begin his sermon.

The adult Bible class thoroughly studied a portion of the book of Luke this morning. The many stories and accounts of Jesus all flooded back to Ethan's memory. Jesus was a wise, strong, and courageous man. A pure example of love as He came down to earth to die for not just Ethan's sins, but for everyone's. Then, He arose and ascended into Heaven to prepare a place for man and God to dwell after man's death. Ethan used to claim the same Jesus as his Savior.

What happened with his walk with the Lord? What used to be a solid walk was now a crumbled and shattered pathway. Ethan had walked away, leaving his life in fragments because he felt he didn't have any hope. He could have held onto God after his parents' tragic deaths, but he didn't. With nothing but a Bible to see his reflection in, Ethan finally saw himself for who he really was without the Lord—a frail human being who thought he could shove everything away and do life on his own. How foolish.

He had been wrong for the past three years. God never left him…he left God. The guilt and realization hit him hard. His last three years could have been amazing had he not let go of God's hand.

Ethan swallowed his dry throat, suddenly feeling nauseous.

Hope placed her small, dainty hand on the top of his rugged one. He didn't deserve to meet a girl who genuinely cared so much about him, but he was appreciative she was placed in his life when he needed someone the most. Hope pushed her way into his life by helping him and showing him the truth, even if he didn't particularly want it. He was falling in love with that fact.

Ethan turned his attention back on the service. Mark placed his Bible on the tall wooden podium in front of him. "If you have your Bibles with you this morning, I'd like for you to turn to Psalm 71. We'll be looking at verses one and two." Mark spoke as he turned the pages in his own Bible.

In all the frantic rushing he'd done this morning, Ethan had forgotten to grab his old Bible. So, Hope shared hers with him throughout the service. He noticed early on that she also noted things in the margins of her Bible. Some of her *i's* were even dotted with hearts. It brought a smile to Ethan's lips as it reminded him of his mom.

The verses Mark began to read popped out to him on the tattered pages of Hope's Bible. She had them highlighted in a pastel pink color. "In thee, O LORD, do I put my trust: let me never be put to confusion. Deliver me in thy righteousness, and cause me to escape: incline thine ear unto me, and save me." Mark looked up from his Bible and peered at the crowd. "The title to the message God has given me is three simple words...*God, save me.*"

"Life's a battle, but the battle can be the Lord's. The struggle may be real, but *so is*

God. God doesn't do anything *to* you, He only does things for you. I have this hope, and that hope is knowing God is in control. We need Him to rescue us! True relief does not come when the problem is resolved, because let's be honest, problems will always be there. True relief comes from an enduring trust and hope in God's salvation. Then, and *only then*, will all of our trials be resolved." Mark paused to catch a breath.

Ethan knew the message Mark spoke wasn't intended to be directed at him, yet he felt every ounce. The weight of Mark's words hit hard, and Ethan knew it must have been God dealing with him in this way. Mark's sermon was meant for Ethan, he recognized.

Firmly gripping the podium, sweat dripped from Mark's brow. "To paraphrase a few verses taken from Psalm 62, God *is* my only rock and salvation. He *is* my defender, and I *shall not be* moved.

"The battle is God's. He's our only hope in a dimly lit world. I claim Him as my salvation. My question to you is this: Are you going to let God save your life? It's as easy as the alphabet. *A*: Admit that you're a sinner.

B: Believe that Jesus Christ is the Son of God. And *C*: Confess that Jesus is your Lord.

"If you feel that tug—If you feel your heart yearning for something more. If you feel the tears threatening to spill from your face. I can tell you this: it's the Holy Spirit. But it's also your choice. Will you, or will you not let God into your heart?" Mark directed his question at the church.

Ethan's heart hammered in his chest so loud he couldn't hear Mark's voice. Ethan's beautiful mom. His unfaithful biological father. The stepdad who cared for Ethan. The car accident. His parents dying in the hospital. Ethan's alcohol addiction. Depression. Every little memory flashed through his mind at a rapid speed.

He knew what he needed to do. He could no longer fight this battle called life alone anymore. His heart thumped even harder in his chest. Life on his own was too much for him to bear. Ethan needed someone besides Hope to bring his problems to. Hope cared, but he could tell he caused her to worry about him more than he wanted her to. He needed Someone to bring everything to, no matter the time or how big the problem was…Someone who wouldn't be terrified of the load.

"Don't be afraid to step out and grab God by the hand. I'll pray with you. The whole church will pray with you, for that matter." Mark paused. "God loves you, and He wants *you*." Mark closed his Bible when he had finished up his sermon. Ethan watched him walk down the few steps of the pulpit to his seat on the front row. Piano music started to softly play, and the congregation stood to sing along to the altar call.

His head spinning in circles, the music faded away to a distant echo. Ethan warily stood with everyone else, and his knees nearly gave out from underneath of him.

Hope gripped his arm tightly to steady him. "Are you okay?" Her worried eyes studied his.

The simple question caused tears to emanate from Ethan's eyes. He couldn't fix his life with his own dirty hands. Before he had time to contemplate the words on his tongue, Ethan let them roll off. "Come pray with me, Hope. God's calling me," he whispered softly.

267

FINDING HOPE

Hope's beautiful green eyes glistened as she nodded. Joyful tears welled up in her eyes and she gripped Ethan's hand in hers. Ethan stepped from the pew to the aisle, hand in hand with Hope, and God took everything from there. His knees hit the floor in front of the wooden altar and Ethan closed his eyes, not caring what other's thought anymore. He hadn't prayed in such a long time. He'd forgotten what it was like to talk to a living, loving, and just God.

God, I come to You humbly today, admitting that I need a Savior. You're my only hope out of wickedness, trouble, and stress. I've messed up too many times to count. I have blamed You for so many things. I was in the wrong. Even if You didn't give me a reason as to why my past was unpleasant, I should have held on to You. I trust You now with my life, Lord. Please, take me back.

Ethan felt a hand gently touch his shoulder and he heard someone kneel beside him. Then another. And another. Others were praying with him. In this very moment, the power of God felt so true and alive as voices cried out to the Lord.

He didn't bother to look around him at the people he suddenly appreciated more than words could describe. He kept his mind focused on the one thing he wanted to get right...his relationship with God. His life depended on it.

I'm a sinner, but Your Word says you still love me. So, please forgive me. Forgive me for my selfishness, my foolishness, and my stubbornness. I choose to live for You from now on. Guide my future and my life. Today, I'm giving everything back to You. Create in me a clean heart, God.

Ethan opened his eyes that dripped with tears. He no longer carried the baggage of his past, for he fully surrendered it to God. His burdens weren't heavy, and he felt overwhelmed with the feeling of joy. Felt like a bird finally being released from its cage. For the first time in a long time, Ethan felt excited. He was beginning a new life, a new chapter, and it was starting out wonderfully.

Thank You, God.

Hope's hand still clutched the inside of his, and Ethan found himself never wanting to let go. His heart burst at the seams as he glanced to his left. She was knelt at the altar beside of him, tears streaming down her face. Her gleaming eyes smiled back at him. "What about now? Are you okay, now?"

He nodded with a smile that felt like it could continue to grow forever. "I'm God's."

She reached over and wrapped her arms around him. Warm and fuzzy, the embrace made Ethan's heart melt. He couldn't help but feel so loved in this very moment. Hope had never stopped caring for him and his soul. She stressed over and over to him what it would be like if he gave his problems to God. She hadn't given up on him, and he immediately thanked God. Ethan finally understood why now. He hadn't been this joyful in years, and it was all because of God's unmerited gift of grace.

sixteen

The number of warm embraces Ethan received after church were too many to count. The church he fretted would judge him actually loved him, and welcomed him in with open arms. Ethan finally felt like a part of something. He seemed to find the puzzle piece he'd been missing.

The Italian restaurant Hope's family had chosen seemed fancy. Beautiful crystal light fixtures dimly lit the back room they all gathered in, and bright art canvases were hung to make the walls burst with color. The service seemed friendly as well. Ethan made note to bring Hope back here one day when it was just the two of them.

Ethan pulled a chair out for Hope to take her seat and she thanked him. He took his coat off and sat down between Hope and Sara. Hope's family had not only invited Ethan to lunch, but Sara too. Ethan's heart warmed at the welcoming gesture Hope's family made for his sister. Not only did Hope's family immediately feel like his own, but it felt like home.

Hope's dad, Steven, and Mark indulged in a conversation about sports and the upcoming Chicago Bears game. Sara, Bri, and Heather were absorbed in a conversation about some sort of fancy shoes on sale at the mall. And Ethan sat there enjoying being around faces that were so lovingly familiar.

Hope nudged Ethan's shoulder and turned to face him. He watched as she observed his face with a grin.

Ethan laughed. "What's that cheesy smile for?"

She shook her head. "I'm just really happy for you." Hope tilted her head as she took a sip of her tea. "God is Good."

Ethan let his cheeks turn red as he fiddled with the straw in his soda. This woman and her smile were going to be his kryptonite, but he didn't mind it as long it was always Hope. She seemed to light up every room she walked into, and Ethan found himself longing for more of her. Before he was able to reply, their waitress came by to take their orders.

"Hope has talked a lot about you." Heather took a bite of her key lime pie and didn't even try to hide her grin. Ethan assumed Brianna took her characteristics after her mom.

"Mom!" Hope protested her mother like a 16-year-old would.

Ethan chuckled at Hope's heated cheeks. "I certainly hope it's been good things," Ethan teased while the others laughed.

"It's nice to actually talk and meet with you in person." Steven smiled genuinely.

Over the past forty-five minutes, Ethan had already grown to immensely respect the unselfish person Hope's father was. He appreciated the fact that Steven was not hard on him as he got to know Ethan. He eased their conversations in smoothly and casually.

"It's been a pleasure, Mr. Lawson. Hope has talked a lot about you guys and how close you all are. It's been lovely to actually be a part of it this afternoon." Ethan told the truth. He would be lying if he said it hadn't been nice to be a part of a group again…to feel completely loved. He recognized it as the change of heart God had given him earlier in the day.

Steven smiled and turned his attention to his wife. "It's about time for my nap, Heather, dear." He patted her hand as he yawned.

"It's not a Sunday if Dad doesn't get his nap," Hope informed Ethan.

"In his defense, it is the day of rest," Mark replied with a laugh.

Heather snickered. "Come on Steven, let's go home." She grabbed her purse and pushed her chair in. "The bill is on us."

"Mom, you don't have to do that," Hope protested with a shake of her head.

"Don't question your parents." Steven crossed his arms.

"You're not that intimidating, but I'll obey." Hope accepted her defeat.

Everyone said their goodbyes to Heather and Steven, and Ethan made for sure to thank them personally.

"I'm going to miss them when they leave in the New Year." Bri sadly smiled as she watched her parents stroll hand in hand toward the register.

"Where are they going next?" Ethan asked.

"Africa," Hope responded whilst she played with the straw inside of her glass of melting ice.

Ethan only nodded. It must be hard telling your parents goodbye for months, especially when they were wandering on foreign land. That's who missionaries were, though. They were trained for the job God especially handed them, and it was for a great cause. He looked at missionaries as heroes that often went unnoticed. They didn't get enough credit as they should.

"Who wants to come over to my place and play Scrabble?" Mark laughed. "I get bored."

"I'm game." Bri's sly smirk told Ethan all he needed to know. She was the one who made the Scrabble games intense. Ethan laughed to himself at his thought.

"Would you like to join us, Sara?" Mark offered.

"I'd love to, but don't be offended if I fall asleep. There were a lot of crying kiddos at work last night." Sara laughed. Ethan's sister looked physically drained, but she hardly ever turned down an offer to do something fun.

"What about you two?" Brianna directed her question toward Hope and Ethan.

Ethan glanced at Hope, then back at Brianna. "We'll have to take a rain check. I have some plans for Hope and me this evening." He scratched his head, hoping

276

Brianna wouldn't have anything to say about it.

Brianna's right eyebrow perked, but she saved her breath. Ethan felt thankful for that silence. Bri almost seemed more curious about the two of them than Hope's older brother, Mark was. Ethan always assumed the brothers were the harder ones to deal with. Apparently, he'd been wrong. Sisters were interesting. At least Hope's was.

Hope grinned. "Sorry guys, the reigning champion will be taking her business elsewhere tonight."

Mark rolled his eyes. "Brag much?"

"You're just jealous," Hope taunted him. The banter between Hope and her siblings was amusing.

"Since I won't be there, good luck, Sara. Do me proud." Hope rose from her chair and patted Sara on the shoulder.

Sara saluted Hope with a laugh. "Aye, Aye, captain."

They all gathered up their belongings and shrugged their heavy winter coats on as they prepared to leave the restaurant. Mark made his way over to Ethan before he left. "Consider me your brother now. I'm proud of you, Ethan. You won't regret the decision you made this morning." Mark slapped him on the back and embraced him in a brotherly-type hug.

"Thank you, Mark. I sincerely appreciate all that you guys have done for me." The thanks weren't near enough, but Ethan would try his best to always express his appreciation toward Hope's family as time went on.

"Anytime." Mark smiled and proceeded to give Hope a hug.

Sara took this time to bury her head in Ethan's shoulder. "I'm so proud of you, Ethan."

Feeling tears build up in his eyes, Ethan sniffled them back and held Sara tight. This was the start of something new with his sister, with Hope and her family, and with God. "Your little brother loves you so much, Sara," he whispered the words into her ear.

At those words, the twinkle in her eyes was hard to miss. In attempt to keep her composure in front of everyone, his sister ruffled Ethan's hair and pulled back. "Have fun today, Ethan." She grinned and grabbed her car keys.

They all said their goodbyes and headed their separate ways.

Ethan and Hope skipped outside hand in hand. He swung their hands back and forth like a kid would as she giggled. Ethan kicked up some snow with his boot and grinned at Hope. "St. Louis is only thirty-five minutes away. Let's go have some fun."

"One double dip hot chocolate ice cream for my lady." Ethan slid into the booth Hope chose for the two of them.

She grinned as a thank you and took the cone.

They made it to St. Louis, Missouri before three, bowled a bit, and made a pitstop at a cute ice cream parlor. Hope couldn't wait to see what Ethan had in mind for the rest of the day. So far, it had been the most thrilling day she'd experienced in a long time. Getting the privilege to witness Ethan give his heart to God this morning had been overwhelming. God answered Hope's prayers right in front of her and it had instantly become a massive faith building block for her. God heard prayers, and He answered them. She would never be able to thank God enough.

Hope planned on taking today one step at a time, letting God guide her steps, not wanting to put too much thought into her day.

"I feel guilty. You let me win." Hope winced at the memory of their bowling match.

"You won fair and square." Ethan held his hands up in defense.

She didn't believe him, but she let it slide. "You didn't get any ice cream. That's not fun." Hope gestured toward his Styrofoam coffee cup.

"I'll stick to my good old cup of joe."

"This ice cream is too good to just have coffee."

"If I want a lick of ice cream, I know whose to steal." He winked. "By the way, I didn't have a clue that hot chocolate was an actual ice cream flavor."

"It was on the menu, so I decided to give it a try." She took a lick to determine if it was a hit or a miss. "Not too shabby." The taste surprised her; it was shocking how on point the flavors could be related back to an actual hot chocolate. The white creamy parts tasted just like the fluffy marshmallows she loved to heap up in her hot cocoa. "I might have just got an idea for this winter's cupcake special." She took another lick, relishing the rich taste. "I owe you one."

"If it's anyone who owes anybody something, it's me." He took a sip of his coffee. "If it had not been for your prayers and encouraging me to move forward...I wouldn't have given my life back to God. I'm positive of that."

Hope smiled. "I know I don't seem serious with an ice cream cone in my hand, but Ethan, that's how God works. I pursue Him, I pray, and I pray, and I pray, and God hears. He also answers. He's faithful."

Ethan nodded. "Thank you."

With his eyes glistening and his guard letting down, Hope saw Ethan for who he really was. The subject on God and Christianity didn't seem tense anymore, and it was like having a conversation with other friends. His softening heart brought out the best of him. "What did you have in mind for the rest of the day?"

"Well, since it used to be a tradition in my family to come down here and look at Christmas lights, I thought it'd be fun to do that with you. But we've got a couple hours before dark, and I still need to buy some Christmas gifts. You game to go shopping?"

"Is that even a question?" Hope laughed as she munched on her cone.

"Which ones?" Ethan held up two pair of earrings.

Hope studied them both. The pair he held in his left hand had silver diamonds, the ones in his right were shiny gold hoops. "Go with the gold ones. Sara has a gold necklace that would go pretty with those." Hope spun the rotating jewelry display case. The jewelry here was exquisite, but also expensive.

Ethan nodded.

At 4:30 in the evening, they made it to a local mall. Hope already achieved checking her mom off her Christmas shopping list, as well as her dad. She purchased her mom a new scarf and a tool set for her dad that Ethan insisted Steven would love. She assumed Ethan was nondescriptly hinting around that he wanted one, so Hope managed to snag Ethan one too without him noticing. Ethan attempted to peek in her bags more than once, but Hope made it a point to keep it a secret.

"What should I get for the gift swap?" When Ethan mentioned a Christmas Eve get-together with Sara as well as Hope and her siblings, Hope couldn't hide the enthusiasm. It would be an entertaining night.

"Sara's wrapping a rock. Don't think too hard." He walked around the jewelry counter and Hope followed him.

Hope threw her head back in laughter. "I really hope Mark gets it. I'd love to see his reaction."

"He would be too nice. He'd probably even display it on his mantle," Ethan snickered.

Ethan purchased Sara's beautiful jewelry and they both walked back into the mall. People frantically shopped all around them for last minute Christmas gifts, but Hope and Ethan took their time as they leisurely strolled.

"Is this low-key our first date?" Hope could tell her question caught Ethan off guard when he whipped his head down to look at her.

She figured it was easier to just ask him then to assume. She didn't want to fool around like she was in high school again. Hope was at the age where she didn't have anything holding her back. Her heart held the desire to be a wife…and eventually a mother someday. She wanted to settle with someone who she felt right with. Between Ethan's newfound faith, and his caring personality, she could grasp a future with him.

"If you would like for it to be." He looked down at her, his eyes softening as a dimple formed in his cheek.

"I think I would." She linked their arms together and leaned her head against his bicep as they walked. "You don't have to hide your smile anymore. Your insides are going to bust." She poked his abdomen.

He laughed at her last comment, letting all his emotions bubble out. "Let's go take some photos to remember this day, then." He nodded toward the photo booth in the middle of the mall.

Hope cringed. It was a cheesy idea, but nonetheless, she agreed.

"I know. I know. Talk about cliché, but I'll make it fun. I promise." He intertwined their pinkies together to reassure her of his promise, and then led her inside the cramped photo booth. "Look, they even have props." Ethan grabbed two Santa hats from the bin of multiple Christmas props to use for the reel of four pictures.

Hope giggled when Ethan placed one of the festive hats on her head.

"It's beginning to look a lot like Christmas!" Ethan sang as he put a hat on as well.

Hope chuckled, then selected the Holiday template with gingerbread men for their pictures. The countdown began. "Smile for the first one, okay?"

"It's hard not to when I'm around you," he admitted through his cheesy grin for the first photo.

The camera flashed, and no doubt it picked up Hope's prominent rosy red blush.

"Now let's do a crazy, stupid one." Ethan crossed his eyes and held his ears, making a monkey face.

Hope stuck her tongue out and gave Ethan bunny ears. "We both look ridiculous." She snorted.

The camera flashed once again.

"Okay, we have two more. What shall we do?" Hope looked down at the bin of props and chuckled as an idea came to her. "I've got one."

"As long as I can come up with the last one," Ethan negotiated.

"Deal." Hope handed him a white beard whilst she put on reindeer antlers.

"Good choice." He spoke through his beard.

Ethan held up jingle bells for the picture as the camera went off. Hope giggled

286

at the picture that revealed on the screen. "Alright, what's your bright idea for the last one?" Hope turned to him.

Ethan toyed through the basket, paying no attention to her question.

Hope's brows scrunched and she stifled a laugh. "What are you looking fo—" Her question was interrupted by Ethan giggling…he was up to something. Hope cocked her head sideways in attempt to see what he was hiding from her.

Unexpectedly, Ethan dangled a green object over their heads, but there was no time to discover what it was as he brought his plump lips to hers and she heard the camera click. Hope could care less about the photo booth anymore. Ethan was kissing her. He moved his right hand around her neck as he deepened the kiss. Her raging emotions calmed but didn't fail to come back to life again with a spark of energy. It was paradise.

She could enjoy the kiss this time, and she would take full advantage of it. Hope rested her dainty hand on Ethan's firm chest and kissed him back. She could feel his heart skipping beats underneath of her hand. He was good at kissing. She would give him that.

Ethan reluctantly pulled back. "Mistletoe." His cheesy grin pleased Hope even more as he dangled the green and red mistletoe in front of her face.

Her cheeks heated, but she relaxed as they both laughed. "Your lips taste like my chocolate cupcakes." Hope bit her lip at the memory of his lips on hers.

He coiled a strand of her hair around his finger. "Yours are a lot like strawberries…with a hint of hot chocolate." He winked.

She leaned her head against his shoulder. "I could get used to that."

"Ditto, my little lobster." His hand rubbed her back.

He earned a shove in the ribs for the nickname. "Let's get our pictures and finish up shopping. I'm ready to look at some Christmas lights."

It took twenty-six minutes to get from St. Louis, Missouri to Belleville, Illinois. Ethan enjoyed simply driving around with Hope, his hand in hers and Christmas music playing in the background. It was something he could get used to…her presence.

He hadn't thought he would kiss her today, but that thought changed back in the photo booth at the mall. Ethan couldn't help himself. She looked beautiful today, and they were both having so much fun. He wanted to remember their first kiss, and after kissing her, he realized he really didn't have to capture it. He would remember that kiss for the rest of his life. It was magical. Hope was magical.

Ethan had plans up his sleeve for tonight. Hope would love the Way of Lights drive through Christmas light display.

The memories hit him like a wave crashing onto the seashore as he drove up to the entrance. Instead of letting it all bubble inside, he let it out. "We used to pile up in a car with all kinds of snacks and blankets and sing carols together when our family came here. Nathaniel used to claim he was a professional Christmas caroler. Sara and I disagreed." Ethan eased the brakes as they waited in line behind other cars. He took this chance to reach in the back seat of his truck to grab blankets and a big tub of holiday popcorn mix for the both of them.

Hope snuggled into one of the quilts. "Memories are good. You can't buy those." She reluctantly let go of his hand to open the popcorn mix.

Ethan smiled as they entered the park full of colorful, mesmerizing lights. The fresh coat of snow on the ground made it feel like they'd just driven into the North Pole. He felt like a kid again tonight. He turned on the local radio station that softly played Christmas tunes.

"The lights are beautiful." Hope kept her eyes glued on the giant nutcrackers out her window.

Ethan took this time to appreciate her, and how beautiful *she* was. Even if the truck was dimly lit, the lights outside framed a silhouette around her body. He wished he had a camera to save this moment with a picture. O*h, how pretty she was*. But it wasn't the looks he was falling in love with, it was her heart; and she was stealing his too.

She turned around to her left and handed him some popcorn. "You're

supposed to be looking at the lights, silly."
She grinned, loving the attention he was
sending her way.

"You're a distraction." He carefully
pressed the gas on the truck to move forward
in the slow line of vehicles.

"Believe me, you are too." She
stopped to admire the brightly lit angel beside
the road, then backed her statement up with
an example. "I was making a cake in the
bakery before I got sick. I was supposed to be
piping *Happy Birthday, Henry* on it. Instead,
I ended up writing *Happy Birthday, Ethan*
with a red heart doodled beside of it."

Ethan erupted in laughter. "So,
you've been thinking about me, eh?" he
pestered.

If they weren't in the dark, Ethan
knew he would be able to see the familiar
blush scrawled on her cheeks. "You seem to
be there in my mind quite often," she
admitted. "Thanks to you, I haven't heard the
end of Bri's teasing. I think she took the cake
home with her and froze it."

"I love your family." He chuckled as he momentarily relaxed his head on the headrest.

Hope beamed. "Really?"

He nodded. "Who wouldn't love your family? It was good to be a part of one today."

"It was nice having you there." Hope flicked a piece of popcorn Ethan's way. It probably wasn't the safest thing to do seeing how he was driving, but he still caught it in his mouth. "I could get used to you being there by my side."

Ethan rubbed the back of her hand with his thumb. His grin felt incredible. "I don't plan on leaving—" he glanced at her. "If you don't mind, of course."

"I couldn't think of anything I'd love more." She smiled as they entered an arch tunnel of lights. "How gorgeous."

"This was always my favorite part." Ethan agreed with her. The light show was stunning.

Hope turned her attention back to him; her tone more serious. "Ethan, God

292

comes first. I don't know what He has in store for our relationship, but I know it will be best with Him in the center."

Now, Ethan couldn't agree more. He watched his life go well with God before, and the moment Ethan let go, it went downhill. He decided he didn't want that again, it was time for God to be first, *always*. "I completely agree."

Hope freckled face radiated. "Please tell me this console folds up into a seat."

Ethan laughed. "It indeed does."

Hope giggled and unbuckled her seatbelt. She folded up the console that once put a barrier between the two of them. She snuggled up close to his side with her quilt.

Ethan kissed her hair that smelled like fresh strawberries. "I'm enjoying this."

"You're spoiling me."

"You love it." He wrapped his right arm around her while his left hand guided the steering wheel.

"I can't deny it." She squeezed his hand. "Have you ever thought about having a family of your own, Ethan?" Her question seemed out of the blue, but he knew the subject would come up eventually if they furthered their relationship.

Ethan sighed. He knew if they ever became serious, Hope would desire children. It was something that scared him. He didn't want his children to ever go through what he had to. Losing parents left a hole—a huge, gaping hole covered with an ugly scar. But that sense of fear had to be faced, and Ethan wanted it to be given to God. If God wanted them to have children, they would have children. "I have."

"And?"

"I would eventually love to be a dad." The statement was entirely accurate. He would love to raise a son of his own, teach him all the things Ethan's birth father never had. He gazed at Hope, a warm feeling overtaking him. "You would make a great mom one day." And that she would. Ethan saw the way she lit up when she was around kids. She had a unique bond with them.

She chuckled. "Could you imagine mini versions of us running around your house?"

"*My* house?" Ethan really enjoyed this.

"Let's just say I *really* admire your kitchen." She looked up at him, biting the inside of her cheek.

He laughed. "I *really* enjoy your meals." He mocked her factual tone of voice.

"I am a good cook," she boasted.

"The kitchen is all yours…as long as I can get some horses and dogs for the property. The kids would love that." He let himself dream of the future. No one could fill the role of being his wife better than Hope Lawson.

She buried her head in his side. "I want to spend forever with you."

Ethan's heart skipped a beat and his cheeks heated. "Let's enjoy these lights before my heart explodes." He rubbed her back as she laughed.

Just then, he recognized this woman as the love of his life.

seventeen

ope slid down further into her duvet cover after she closed her memory journal and put away her pen. The grin was impossible to wipe off her face tonight. She glanced at the reel of pictures on her nightstand from the photo booth earlier today.

Ethan kissed her.

She hadn't let that fully register in her mind yet, and now she had time to. The kiss this time wasn't something she regretted. It was one she would treasure for a lifetime. It wasn't the same feeling she received with other guys in the past. This one was different. This kiss felt right, and special. Hope felt like she was on the brink of something magnificent.

Lord, where do I begin? You sent Your Son to die for me. You've given me a lovely family. I asked for a bakery, and You gave it to me. I have prayed diligently for Ethan's soul, and now he's one of Yours again. I am overwhelmed with gratitude.

I'm beginning to sense something between Ethan and I that was meant for more than just friendship. He's a wonderful friend, but I think he's supposed to be more than that in my life. God, he has an amazing heart and cares deeply for others…and ultimately, he cares for You now. Is he the one*? If I'm wrong, tell me. Either way, please guide Ethan's footsteps. Lead him in Your ways, and always protect him.*

Thank You, God, for today. I really needed it.

Ethan woke early Monday morning. He sought to start his rededicated life to God out right. He had watched the sun come up in his living room and felt the warmth in his heart tingle straight to his toes. He even read his Bible this morning while he drank his coffee. He felt like a brand-new person. Ethan respected the man he was with God by his side.

He shivered as snow flurried around him. It was almost below zero degrees today, but Ethan wanted to settle something that he never finished. It was time. He needed to move on.

As he studied this morning, if Jesus forgave those that tortured Him on the cross, Ethan could forgive his birth father, Peter. It was a subject that Ethan had always been sensitive of. He never possessed the desire to forgive someone that had been so cruel not only Ethan, but his family. But today, as he read the story of Jesus' crucifixion, he realized he needed a change of heart. If God could forgive someone as filthy as Ethan used to be, Ethan would choose to forgive Peter. And it was indeed God who laid that desire upon his heart.

Peter was buried in a private gravesite. Not more than ten people were buried with his father. Ethan found Peter's headstone and knelt to brush off the pile of snow built up on the grey stone.

Peter Wallace. Never a man big on words. He was someone Ethan had looked up to, until Ethan was old enough to realize his dad wasn't the best example. Peter had somehow gotten lost down life's winding road, just like Ethan had. But Peter did not get the second chance that Ethan was mercifully given. God's grace stepped in for Ethan, and he couldn't express his gratitude to the Lord enough.

The four words that Ethan had never been able to say, now rolled off his tongue easily. "I forgive you, Dad." Ethan placed the bouquet of crimson roses by Peter's headstone and quietly walked away. The relief of emotions were incredible as he felt a barrier break in his life.

Thank You, God. Thank You for Your grace.

eighteen

Hope retrieved the bubbling chicken casserole from Ethan's scorching hot oven. "Dinner's ready!" She took two plates out of the cabinet for her and Ethan.

It was Tuesday evening and Ethan sat somewhere in his stepdad's old office, still job hunting. Hope grinned. Ethan had no idea about the news she carried with her this evening. She hummed along with the old record player that she brought into Ethan's kitchen, feeling ecstatic.

Ethan's kitchen. It easily became her favorite place to hang out in his home. She tested out a new cupcake recipe last night with Ethan in here and succeeded. Hope hungrily desired for the day this kitchen would be hers. She also wanted Ethan to be hers. He enjoyed her food, so she thought of it as a win-win situation. Hope chuckled at the thought.

"It smells delicious." Ethan snaked his arms around her waist and placed a kiss atop her hair.

"Any luck?" Hope continued preparing their plates. She piled the green beans on her plate, they were her favorite.

He snatched a bean off her plate. "No." His rough voice groaned.

"It will come." She bit back the smile to keep her secret hidden for now.

"I know." He leaned against the counter.

"Let's eat." She handed him his plate, and they sat down at the round dinner table in the dining room.

Hope admired the bright yellow color as she sliced the delectable looking lemon meringue pie. She really needed to sell more pies in her bakery, her customers would go crazy for them.

Hope cut two pieces of the pie and placed them on Ethan's mother's delicate dessert plates. Their light conversation and meal had been nice earlier this evening. Evenings like this with Ethan were enjoyable, but Hope couldn't contain her secret for much longer. Her insides bubbled with anticipation from the news she had waiting for him.

"I'm getting spoiled." Ethan looked up from the newspaper he'd been reading and chuckled as Hope handed him a piece of pie.

She plopped down on the couch beside him. With a stab of her fork into the buttery smooth dessert, Hope entered dessert ecstasy.

"What's up with you?" Ethan nudged her side with a curious smile.

Hope swallowed a taste of the tart dessert. "What do you mean?"

"You've been acting weird today." He pointed his fork at her. "You're up to something," Ethan stated after he took another bite.

"What makes you say that?"

"You're biting your lip. That's why." Ethan wiped meringue off the corner of Hope's mouth.

Hope stopped her nervous habit in an instant, deciding it was time to tell him. "I've been doing a little job hunting for you." She dramatically paused and Ethan patiently waited for her to continue. "I got to talking with Mark. There are no jobs available at the station, but he went to the board of education for me to look for job openings. I figured the chances were slim, seeing how it's the middle of the year and all but…"

"But what?" Hope successfully captured Ethan's full attention.

"We decided to check anyways." She nonchalantly shrugged as she ate another mouthful of the pie.

"*And?*"

303

Hope laughed at his growing impatience. "The middle school is in desperate need of a gym instructor. The previous teacher gave the position up due to a better job offer. No one wants the position. It's all yours if you want it. You get first dibs because of previous experience."

Ethan dropped his fork on his plate, creating a clattering sound. "You're kidding!" His mouth stood open in awe.

Hope's heart fluttered rapidly at his reaction. "I've seen you around kids, Ethan. You should really consider the position."

"How did you manage this?" Elated, and not knowing what to do with himself, he tickled Hope's feet. All he wanted to do was kiss her pretty face.

"I know a guy." She casually shrugged her shoulders and added a smirk. "If you take the job, they would want you to start right after Christmas break ends. And there's something else…"

"There's more?" He was already speechless. How could she possibly have more news?

Hope laughed with a nod of her head. "In the spring, the high school wants to offer you a coaching position for the soccer team."

Her words echoed in his head, and Ethan didn't know whether to believe Hope or not. Surely it was a setup or some sort of joke. But when Hope didn't say anything else, Ethan's head dropped to his hands, propped on his knees with his elbows. His posture collapsed as tears streamed down his face. All the joy bubbled and spilled out. "God, I'm overwhelmed." He choked the words out.

Being the coach of a soccer team before he'd selfishly quit, Ethan realized then that this was truly a second chance for something he had a passion in. This time he was being offered so much more. *A physical education teacher.* He could see himself being one, especially to middle school children.

God, You are wonderful.

Hope placed her hand on his knee. "So, what do you say...are you going to take it?"

Ethan gazed into her compassionate smile and he nodded. "Thank you, Hope. There's no way I can deny that amazing opportunity."

Hope clapped her hands together with a squeal. "Merry early Christmas, Ethan Grey." She grinned.

Ethan pulled her good-looking face close to his and kissed her soft lips. Her lips tasted like cake batter this evening. She bought a new Chapstick. Ethan playfully took note of that and stashed it away with the rest of his mental notes filed under *Hope*.

He decided to seize this opportunity to tell her how he really felt. Ethan would have fun with this. "Knock, Knock."

Hope giggled and cuddled up close to him. "I thought the jokes were mine."

"Just give me this one." He pouted his lips.

She laughed and finally agreed. "Who's there?"

"I."

"I, who?" He could tell just how cheesy the joke was going to be when he watched her bite back a laugh.

He tickled Hope's ribs and continued with his comedy session. "I love you." Ethan meant those small, yet powerful three words that made his heart hammer against his chest.

Hope's cheeks flashed a bright red color as tears brimmed her eyes. "I love you more, Ethan." She chuckled at his cheesiness.

Ethan shook his head in disagreement with her statement. "I love you most." He closed the small gap in between them and placed another gentle kiss on her lips.

"That was a good joke." Hope grinned as they pulled apart.

He pulled her onto his lap to stroke her silky strawberry-blonde hair. "Not a joke, but I thought it was a good one."

nineteen

"You're falling in love." Brianna smiled genuinely at Hope as she peered over her glass of water.

Hope and her sister were out for lunch on their break. It was the least she could do after leaving Brianna in charge of the bakery last week when Hope had been sick. Plus, it felt refreshing to chat with just her sister. "We're past the falling stage...I've fallen quite a million times already. I'm just plain in love with him now." Hope admitted and took a bite of her delicious club sandwich, relishing Patti's Diner.

Her sister chuckled. "I like Ethan, and so do Mom and Dad."

Hope choked on her sandwich. "You do a lot of talking, don't you?"

"I get around." Bri shrugged, that familiar sly grin beginning to grow on her lips again. "Ethan's good for you."

Hope laughed. "Your concern for me is appreciated."

"I wouldn't be much of a sister if I wasn't concerned, now would I?"

Rolling her eyes, Hope grinned at the mulling thought in the back of her head. "Now...all we need to do is find you a guy." She paused and coughed out the next words. *"Brandon Smith."*

Brianna snarled her nose. "Brandon David Smith will never be an option. Mark my words. My single life is going just fine. Although, I'm beginning to realize that dogs are fun. I like Mark's puppy." Brianna considered it, veering off the subject purposefully.

"That mutt chewed my shoe to pieces last time I visited. I bought him a toy for Christmas to shred instead." Hope now needed new boots.

"He's too precious to correct." Brianna made pitiful excuses for the dog.

Hope laughed, agreeing with her sister. "Mark needs a wife. Someone to support his dreams and passions."

Bri nodded. "He's getting lonely. I want to see him settle down and be happy."

Hope agreed. Whoever Mark married would be the luckiest woman in the world. Mark had a gushy heart full of sweetness that could make a girl drool. "You like to play matchmaker. Set him up."

"He would resent me." Bri took a sip of her hot chocolate with a roll of her eyes.

The two sisters finished up their lunches and waited for the waitress to bring them their bill. "After Christmas, I'm bringing out the winter cupcake of the month..." She drummed her fingers on the table. "Hot chocolate." Hope waggled her jazz fingers.

"Sounds delicious. Where'd you get the idea?" Brianna pulled her coat on as their bill was brought to the table.

"Well, one: everyone especially loves hot chocolate this time of year. Two: Ethan bought me an ice cream in that flavor and let's just say it was to die for." Hope grabbed her wallet to pay for their lunch, and Bri payed the tip.

"I can't wait to try it." Brianna pushed her chair in as Hope rose to get ready to leave.

"I attempted trial recipe number one and two at Ethan's place the other night. He declared they both needed more marshmallow crème and cocoa."

"Men. You can't please them," Brianna huffed.

"I guess I have some more tweaking to do." Hope laughed and opened the door for her sister.

Brianna hopped in the passenger's seat. "Back to the bakery we go"

"Brian loved his superhero cake. You should have seen his reaction. It was priceless." Ethan helped Hope box cranberry almond cupcakes for a delivery later that afternoon.

Ethan volunteered himself as extra help around the bakery until Christmas break for public schools were over. He was often on delivery duty with Funfetti's new delivery man, Marcus. Although, Ethan managed to purposefully stumble into the kitchen and Hope's cupcakes often. Hope appreciated the handsome distraction, nonetheless.

"I'm glad. His mom seemed pretty adamant about doing all his favorite superheroes and not just a single one. Seems like it worked out." She smiled and handed him a tray of leftover cupcakes from the order. "Hand these to either Laney or Ashley. They're fresh batches for the display case."

"Okie dokie." He whistled and headed toward the door to the café.

Hope watched him walk away and smiled to herself. Ethan had come so far. His usual pessimistic and dark attitude from two months ago was now something odd and peculiar when one was around him. It was rare when she didn't see him smiling with his two dimples prominent. Ethan seemed at home when he was at peace with God.

Ethan hadn't changed for Hope. He changed for God. That fact was confirmed to

Hope through his actions and new way of life. Monday, he left a letter in Hope's coat pocket expressing how greatly he appreciated her. Last night, he called her just to pray with her before bed. It was the little things that seemed so unimportant to others that Hope wouldn't forget.

"You're blushing." Jade maneuvered through the kitchen with a hot pan of strawberry cream cheese croissants in hand.

"Am I?" Hope laughed. "Your croissants smell heavenly." She followed her employee to sample one.

"My grandmother's old recipe. I decided to give them a whirl." The young girl handed Hope half of a croissant to try. "Be honest with me." She bit her lip waiting in anticipation for Hope's reaction.

Hope sank her teeth into the warm croissant and her taste buds danced. The gooey strawberry filling and cream cheese on top stuck to her fingers as she took another bite. "These are delicious, Jade! I want them on the menu. People will go crazy over these yummy treats."

Jade's worried frown turned into an elated smile. "Thank you."

"Of course." Hope grinned and rushed to clean her hands up at the sink before she started to work at her station again.

Since it was Christmas Eve, busy customers bustled in and out of her bakery to buy last minute desserts for dinners and gettogethers. It was nice business and she had been enjoying her day, but Hope couldn't wait for this evening. She would get off work, rush home to grab a shower and get ready, then go to Ethan's place for their gettogether with their siblings.

Hope believed Ethan was experiencing an unforgettable Christmas season after his past three years of depression. She knew from her personal life; the holidays were unforgettable when she had loved ones that warmly welcomed her in and cared for her. But it was Ethan's change of heart and relationship with God that made this Christmas one of the best Christmases...even for Hope. Ethan understood now that Christmas was special because of Jesus Christ. It wasn't about what was under the tree, it was the people surrounding them. And this year, Hope felt even more appreciative of life and loved ones.

The pastel pink kitchen door swung open and Ethan sauntered back in the kitchen, stuffing a whole cupcake in his mouth. Hope found him attractive even with his cheeks plum full of cake and frosting.

"I asked you to give them the cupcakes, not eat them all." Hope poked his cheeks as he finished the cupcake with a gulp. "You look like a squirrel."

"They'll never know that one went missing." He stated matter-of-factly as he licked his fingers clean of frosting.

Hope scrunched her nose at Ethan's messy hands and urged him to wash them. "Unless they know how to do math," she teased him and rolled out white fondant for a new cake order.

Ethan picked up where he left off on boxing goodies. "Listen, I have to stop by the school to drop off my lesson plans after we're done here. Do you just want me to swing by your place and pick you up for our Christmas Eve extravaganza?" He put an exciting

315

emphasis on the word *extravaganza* and his eyes lit up like a Christmas tree.

"Oh, so now it's an extravaganza?" Hope looked up at him with a raised eyebrow.

He smirked. "I know how to throw a good party."

"We're a party of five, Ethan."

"And if it were a party of two, it would still be an extravaganza." He pointed an iced sugar cookie at Hope, his eyebrows narrowed.

Hope chuckled. "You're cute." She paused from trimming the smooth fondant. "You can pick me up, but no complaining if I'm not ready on time." The school wasn't far from Hope's apartment. So, it wouldn't be too out of Ethan's way for him to pick her up.

Ethan held his hands up in defense. "I won't argue with the baker."

"I brought my dog." Mark tattled on himself as he stomped the snow off his boots before entering Ethan's home.

Hope laughed at the squirming puppy inside of her brother's coat. "It's a good thing Ethan loves animals."

Mark sat the dog down and Snoopy began to explore the unfamiliar territory.

"How was work today?" Hope took Mark's heavy coat and placed it on a silver hanger by the door.

"Long." He sighed. "We've had three houses broken into in the past week. It's been busy at the station recently. We expect that, though, with Christmas just around the corner."

Between Mark's weary eyes and the defined lines etched on his face, Hope could tell he hadn't received much sleep in the past twenty-four hours. "God gave you this job because He knew you could handle it. He gives strength." Snoopy jumped at Hope's heels for attention. Hope reached down to pet the dog's golden locks. "I believe in you, big bro. You'll catch them."

Mark smiled as a thank you and enveloped Hope in a warm hug. "Where is everyone? I expected an *extravaganza*," he mocked.

317

Hope blinked back a grin.

"Ethan's words, not mine."

"The extravaganza—party of five, now that you're here—is in the kitchen. Probably eating all the food."

"We can't have that. I'm starved. Brandon ate half my sandwich for lunch."

Hope chuckled. "There are sub sandwiches, soups, meatballs, and plenty of desserts." She led her brother into the kitchen filled with laughter and delicious smelling foods.

"Mark!" Instantly, he was greeted with friendly smiles and hugs. Hope watched his tired frown turn into a smile that not only lifted his spirits up, but Hope's as well. She didn't like it when her brother felt grim.

Ethan made Mark at home by grabbing him a soda and showing him where all the foods were. Hope smiled as she settled into a kitchen chair and listened to everyone talk. Sara and Brianna were debating on which color to paint Sara's kitchen, as Ethan proved to Mark that siracha sauce was delicious on anything.

Hope treasured this. Being with people she loved, knowing they loved her back, made her heart all fuzzy and warm. She wished she could freeze time and stay right in this moment—A moment filled full of love and happiness that she could look back on or revisit when bad days came occasionally. But since she couldn't, Hope would write about it in her memory journal tonight when she got home.

God, Your love is unexplainable. Thank You for all You have given me. I don't deserve it, yet somehow, You have handed it to me anyway. For that, I just want to say thank You. Waiting was worth it for this moment in time. I feel You all around me, and I know I'm right where I belong. I truly believe this is the foundation of something remarkable. Whatever You decide to do with Ethan and I, I will fully put my trust in Your plan. Guide us, Lord, into this new, exciting adventure called our lives.

"Whatcha' thinking about?"

Hope blinked back to reality and looked up to see Ethan standing in front of her. Everyone must have gone into the living room, for the kitchen was now bare and quiet.

319

She smiled at him and took in his presence. He smelled of a new, musky, fresh cologne. Hope admired it. The hooded sweatshirt he wore was a new one the school had given him in honor of taking the gym teacher position. It was newer than the old one he let her borrow tonight, but she wouldn't tease him about it. His hair was undone, and he seemed comfortable. By the gorgeous smile on his face, he looked genuinely happy tonight.

"How much I love you…" She responded and paused to look around. "And this."

He rubbed her shoulders. "We have pretty cool siblings, don't we?"

"We make a good team." Hope smiled and took a drink of her Coke that had gone flat.

"You're the fruit to my loop." Ethan's cheesy grin told Hope he was proud of his lovey dovey joke.

Hope giggled at him and stood up from her chair. "I want your cheesy jokes for the rest of my life. They get me pumped for my standup comedy career that I'm going to take up one day."

Ethan threw his head back with a laugh and embraced her in a long, tingling hug. She loved this strong man. His life had been put through the wringer more than once, and Hope desired to be by his side forever, even when things got tough. She snuggled her right cheek against his chest, and he settled his chin on the top of her head.

"I plan on waking you up every day with my corny jokes." He gently rubbed circles at the small of her back. "Did you know that you look really good in my hoodie?"

Hope could see the smirk on his face without having to look up at him. "I was just cold."

He snickered. "Don't make up excuses." Ethan kissed her forehead. "Come on, it's time for the gift swap. I'm praying Mark gets my gift. It's better than Sara's."

"Why is that?" Hope interlaced her fingers with his warm ones.

"Funny you should ask. You mentioned he loved animals...right?"

321

Hope looked up at Ethan's face to see if he was serious.

He was.

"I've officially met Snoopy. I've decided Snoopy needs a best friend."

Hope exploded in laughter.

twenty

Ethan watched Mark grab the gift that aligned with the slip of paper Mark held in his hand. By the sly smile on Sara's face when Mark picked up the gift, Mark had drawn her number. Ethan chuckled to himself. Poor Mark.

Ethan was first to open his gift. He had drawn Mark's name. His gift consisted of a basket filled to the brim with assorted candies, candy bars, and gift cards. Mark knew how to buy gifts, and Ethan happily appreciated it. Ethan imagined he was going to get fat before he started his new job.

Getting concerned about who had drawn his number, Ethan restlessly shifted in his seat. He'd hoped that Mark would draw Ethan's gift's number, because Ethan got Mark a puppy. Watching Mark go back to his seat with Sara's gift in hand, Ethan realized his plan clearly backfired on him. The puppy wasn't something he invested money in, though. A teacher at the middle school was giving one away. He naturally thought it would be a clever idea. Just as his luck went…nothing worked out as planned.

Would any of the girls want a dog? If not, Ethan would gladly take the puppy. The golden doodle was too cute to return or get rid of.

He was astonished the dog hadn't yipped yet. It had been patiently waiting in Ethan's bedroom and had surprisingly been quiet all evening. He had managed to slip some food to the excited little pup while everyone had been eating and talking earlier. Ethan's stomach did backflips as the anticipation ate at him.

Grunting, Mark settled back into the soft leather chair and opened his heavy gift. He laughed once he realized why the gift was so heavy. "Who got this?" He scanned the room with a suspicious gaze.

Sara raised her hand. "Guilty." She laughed.

Mark held up the perfectly round miniature boulder. "How thoughtful of you." He chuckled.

"I couldn't stand the thought of just getting someone a rock. The real gift is hidden under the couch," Ethan's sister admitted and got up from her seat to retrieve her real gift.

Ethan laughed. His sister was too nice.

"Now why's that? A rock is a perfect way to say Merry Christmas," Mark teased.

"Well, you can frame the rock, but I insist you open up a real gift." Sara handed him the perfectly wrapped gift.

Mark laughed and accepted the present. Everyone watched as he unwrapped the gift from Sara. Hope's brother gasped, "Oh, my goodness. This isn't…" Once he made for sure what it was, Mark hugged the gift like a child.

"What is it?" Brianna threw a wad of wrapping paper in Mark's direction.

Mark proudly showed off his new prized possession. "It's a limited-edition Scrabble game."

Hope chuckled at her brother's starstruck expression. "You know that means it's just another game for me to beat you at, right?"

Mark shot his sister an *I'll accept that challenge* look, then thanked Sara for the gift.

"He's jealous." Hope leaned into Ethan's arms.

Ethan snickered. "Sara, you're up next."

With no hesitation, his sister jumped up from the couch and picked her gift with the right number on it. "Ooo, let's see." She began ripping open the paper once she sat back down.

"If you don't like it, you can return it." Brianna nervously chewed on her nails as she watched Ethan's sister open the gift.

Sara squealed and Snoopy barked at her sudden excitement. "I love it!" Sara pulled out a Polaroid camera and extra film.

"Brianna, thank you." She reached over and gave Bri a squeeze.

Ethan anxiously bit his lip. Either Hope or Brianna would be receiving Miss Fluffypup tolerantly waiting in his bedroom. His plans weren't going down how he'd originally drawn them up, but Ethan chose to have some fun with it.

Brianna skipped to retrieve her numbered gift and Ethan eyed her carefully. And when she didn't pick up Ethan's empty box, he laughed to himself. Hope would be getting the puppy. She was in for a real treat.

Brianna opened her gift from Hope. It held a basket full of face masks, nail polish, and all sorts of girly things.

"I'm really glad that a girl received my gift. I couldn't bear to go through the misery of perusing the men's section. Girly stuff is more fun for me," Hope admitted with a grin.

Brianna chuckled at her sister's comment and dug through the box of unending pink things. "I love it. Thank you." She smiled at Hope.

327

"Okay, there's one more gift under the tree," Mark announced.

"Hope, you're the only one left. Go get your gift." Sara motioned, excited for her.

Hope hopped up out of Ethan's arms. She reached for the box that Ethan placed under the tree as his little disguise. "Wow, for such a big, pretty red box it's really airy."

That's because it was. The box was empty other than a miniature stuffed animal in the bottom. He prayed Hope recollected their conversation earlier about his gift. Maybe she would think of it as a joke and Ethan would then surprise her. He couldn't wait for Hope's reaction.

"I assume this is from you." She smiled ruefully in Ethan's direction.

"Your guess would be correct." He nodded as he took a sip of his coffee, trying to seem as nonchalant as possible.

She untied the silver bow and lifted the lid to the box. Hope doubled over in laugher when she spied the stuffed dog at the bottom of the gift box. "I get it now," she hooted.

Oh, but she didn't. Ethan wanted to roll on the floor and laugh. Instead it all bubbled inside and his cheeks hurt from smiling. "Hold that thought. I'll be right back." He jogged up to his bedroom and cracked open the wooden door. The tiny golden puppy jumped at Ethan's heels.

Lord, please don't let there be any messes.

He breathed a heavy sigh of relief as he examined the room, realizing the dog hadn't used the bathroom or thrown up anywhere. Ethan knelt to pet the excited puppy. "Hi, girl. Let's go meet your owner." The pup licked Ethan's hand and he chuckled. If he married Hope, this dog would be theirs. He found himself liking that idea very much.

Ethan hid the squirming puppy in his sweatshirt. The entire process to this surprise was too amusing. He walked backwards into the living room. "I need Hope to close her eyes and open her hands up."

"On it." He heard Mark reply and footsteps pitter-patter across the living room to the couch Hope relaxed in. Ethan heard a giggle from the woman he loved.

329

"Okay, she's ready," Brianna informed Ethan.

Ethan turned around to see Mark covering Hope's eyes and he laughed at the scene. He would remember this moment forever. He pulled the fidgeting puppy from his sweatshirt and heard gasps and giggles from everyone whose eyes were open. Sara pulled her Polaroid camera out and positioned herself to take a picture.

"On the count of three, Hope, you can open your eyes," Ethan instructed her. "Now, if you don't like this gift, there's no receipt...so, you better like it."

Mark laughed at Ethan's worried statement.

"Okay," she replied to him in a high-pitched giggle. She seemed as excited as a child on Christmas morning.

"One..." Ethan stroked the puppy that was too eager to meet its owner.

"Two..." He slowly lowered the puppy right above Hope's hands.

Snoopy barked and yipped at the sight of another dog that could potentially be his new best friend. "Three!" A camera flashed as Hope opened her eyes, snapping her flabbergasted reaction and Ethan's enormous grin.

"You really did get an animal!" Hope snickered as the puppy licked her face. "Ethan, oh my! I love her." She sank into the couch and let the dog lick her all over.

Ethan watched as Hope's smile seemed to grow larger by the minute. "You won't be getting any kisses from me with slimy doggy kisses all over you." Ethan chuckled and settled down beside of her.

"How in the world did you manage this?" his sister asked him from across the couch.

"I know a guy." He proudly smirked as he shrugged his shoulders.

Ethan poured a cup of piping hot coffee for him, and a cup of jasmine tea for Hope.

The house was empty and quiet now, except for Hope and her dog. Tonight's Christmas gettogether couldn't have gone

331

any more perfect. It had been wonderful to see their families gather together and be as one. It was a type of fun that didn't require getting wasted. Ethan experienced love and the excitement of being a part of a Christian group again. It was something that made his soul rejoice.

He carefully made his way back to his living room with the two mugs and took a seat beside Hope. She happily accepted her cup of tea and rested her head on the headrest of the couch. "I loved the look on Mark's face when he unwrapped the rock."

"It was priceless," Ethan agreed with a chuckle. "You know what else was priceless?"

Hope beamed, already knowing the answer. "I had no idea I would be getting a dog tonight." She carefully caressed the small puppy curled up in her lap. "I decided on the name Maya. I thought it was cute."

"Surprises are fun. I like the name, by the way." Ethan ruffled the puppy's curly fur. "I got to thinking, Maya can be *our* dog."

Hope laughed and brushed her bangs to the side. "You're quite attached to her already, huh?"

"Indeed I am." He took a taste of his steaming coffee. "I know a simple way to settle this...how we can both have her."

"How's that?" She seemed to hold her breath.

Ethan took hold of Hope's dainty left hand. "What about putting a ring on this finger?" He pointed to her ring finger. "What about marrying me?" Ethan's curious gaze met hers.

Hope grinned from ear to ear as her emerald eyes glistened. Ethan loved Hope more than he could ever find words to describe. He would love to spend year after year endlessly chasing after Hope's beautiful heart.

She bit her lip and nodded with a smile. "Can we elope?"

"I think the quicker, the better." He chuckled and squeezed her hand, taking her reply as a yes.

"Only thing is, my dad won't like not getting to walk his daughter down the aisle." Hope maneuvered herself and the dog, so she could lay her head in Ethan's lap.

"He can meet us at the courthouse." Ethan winked at her.

Hope giggled and played with Ethan's fingers, and Ethan traced the freckles perfectly aligned by God on Hope's face. How had he gotten this lucky?

God. He answered his own question.

Hope was going to make the loneliness of this big house disappear. He couldn't wait to come home to her gorgeous smile, to make her cinnamon rolls on Sunday mornings, to take her to church. It was the small things that would change that excited him the most. It was time for a new chapter, and Ethan found himself more than willing to move on with God and Hope by his side. It was a solid foundation, an overwhelming start. And it was absolutely thrilling.

Ethan inhaled a deep breath. "I've wasted three years of my life, Hope. And I believe God sent me you in the lowest time of my life for a purpose. He knew that I felt

334

so alone and heartbroken. So, He sent me hope, quite literally." They both laughed at his comment. "Hope we have as an anchor of the soul." He smiled as he quoted the familiar Scripture from the book of Hebrews.

He wiped a tear with his thumb that escaped from the corner of Hope's eye. "Through you obeying God, I now have a relationship with Him on my own. I don't ever want to lose that again. So, I just want to simply say this…thank you, Hope." He exhaled as a tear fell from his own eye. "I want to spend the rest of my life chasing your exquisite golden heart."

Hope sighed heavily, seeming to ponder each word he said. "God is faithful." She whispered and closed her eyes as another happy tear rolled down her cheek. "I love you so much, Ethan." Hope kissed the back of Ethan's hand.

"I'll love you always." He kissed her nose and she smiled.

Ethan played with her slick strawberry-blonde hair that had originally attracted him in the first place. Well, that…and the freckles. "Hope Lawson, I just thought you would like to know that you have stolen my heart."

She blushed and closed her eyes. "That's okay, I'll just steal your last name." She winked with a smirk beginning to form at the corner of her mouth.

Ethan laughed as he gently stroked Hope's hand with the back of his thumb. He was going to love this woman for the rest of his lifetime, then he'd spend an eternity with her and God in Heaven. Never had he experienced so much hope in one moment.

Double Chocolate Chip Muffins

What You'll Need:

- ¾ cup of brown sugar
- ⅓ cup of vegetable oil
- 6 tablespoons of unsweetened cocoa powder
- 6 tablespoons of hot water
- 2 eggs
- 2 teaspoons of vanilla extract
- 1 ⅔ cups of all-purpose flour
- 2 teaspoons of baking powder
- ½ teaspoons of baking soda
- ¼ teaspoons of salt
- ¾ cups of sour cream or Greek yogurt, heaping

- 1⅓ cups of semisweet chocolate chips (or a mix of regular and mini)

Instructions:

1. Preheat oven to 400 degrees Fahrenheit. Line a standard size muffin tin with liners.
2. In a large mixing bowl combine the sugar and oil. Beat on high for 2 minutes. Combine cocoa and hot water in a small bowl, whisk until smooth. Add to sugar and oil, beat for 1 minute. Add eggs and vanilla, mix until combined.
3. In a different mixing bowl, whisk flour, baking powder, baking soda and salt. Gradually alternate adding the dry ingredients and sour cream or yogurt to the large mixing bowl. Don't overmix! Fold in 1 cup of the chocolate chips with a spatula.
4. Using a large scoop, scoop up the muffin batter and fill each liner. Sprinkle the remaining ⅓ cup of chocolate chips on top and gently press into batter. Bake for 7 minutes, then reduce heat to 350 degrees Fahrenheit and continue baking for 10-12 more minutes. Cracks should appear slightly moist and edges should be firm. Remove from oven

and allow to cool in the pan for 5 minutes before transferring to a wire rack to cool completely.

5. Enjoy Ethan's all-time favorite!

Mixed Berry Streusel Muffins

What You'll Need:

- 2 cups of sugar
- 2 cups of self-rising flour
- 2 cups of milk
- Splash of vanilla
- 1 cup of blueberries
- 1 cup of strawberries
- 1 cup of blackberries and/or raspberries (optional)
- 1 stick of butter, melted
- 1/3 cup of light-brown sugar
- 2 tablespoons of all-purpose flour
- 2 tablespoons of butter
- ½ teaspoons of ground cinnamon
- ½ cup of packed light brown sugar
- 1 ½ teaspoon of ground cinnamon

Instructions:

1. Preheat oven at 350 degrees Fahrenheit.
2. Mix sugar and flour together. Add milk, vanilla, and butter.
3. Pour batter in Texas-size muffin pan (pre-lined with cupcake liners) and sprinkle desired berries into muffin cups in batter.
4. In a bowl, combine the 1/3 cup of brown sugar, 2 tablespoons of flour, and ½ teaspoon of ground cinnamon. Add the 2 tablespoons of butter in tablespoon size increments, then cut it into mixture and mix. Sprinkle the streusel on top of batter and bake for 25 minutes. Pull out of oven.
5. Combine ½ cup of packed light brown sugar and 1 ½ teaspoon of ground cinnamon and sprinkle on almost finished muffins. Place back in oven for 5-10 more minutes or until toothpick comes out clean and edges are golden. Top with fresh berries.
6. Indulge in Ethan's amazing new concoction!

Apple Streusel Bread

"Ethan's Thanksgiving Alternative"

What You'll Need:

- ½ cup of packed light brown sugar
- 1 ½ teaspoon of ground cinnamon
- 2/3 cup of white sugar
- ½ cup of butter (softened)
- 2 eggs
- 2 teaspoons of vanilla extract
- 1 ½ cups of all-purpose flour
- 1 ½ teaspoons of baking powder
- ½ cup of milk
- 1 large apple (peeled and finely chopped)

Instructions:

1. Preheat oven to 350 degrees Fahrenheit.

2. Grease and flour a 9 x 5-inch loaf pan.
3. Mix brown sugar and cinnamon together in a bowl and set aside.
4. With a mixer, combine white sugar and butter until smooth.
5. Add eggs and vanilla to mixing bowl and beat on medium speed until combined evenly.
6. Add flour and baking powder, then milk.
7. Pour half of batter into the loaf pan you prepared earlier. Cover that with half of your apples. Pat apples into batter with the back of a spoon. Sprinkle that with half of cinnamon-brown sugar mixture.
8. Pour the remaining batter over apple layer; top with remaining apples and more of the cinnamon mixture. Pat topping into batter with the back of a large spoon.
9. Bake for around fifty minutes or until a toothpick inserted comes out clean.
10. Enjoy Ethan's Thanksgiving alternative!

Dear Reader,

Thank you so much for reading *Finding Hope*. I absolutely fell in love with the story of Hope and Ethan. I am honored to be able to share this inspirational romance with you.

Being my first book, I must thank God for this amazing opportunity. He laid upon my heart to write about hope, so I literally did. *Finding Hope* brings Hebrews 6:19 to life. No matter the condition and shape you are in right now, God will welcome you in with open arms. He casts your sin as far as the east is to the west. He loves you. He cares deeply for you. He would love nothing more than to have a relationship with you and give you Heaven. Anchor in that hope.

Not only did I learn that throughout writing this book, but I also learned that God lets things happen in our lives not to destroy us, but to make us stronger, better people. Things happen, and sometimes they're unexplainable, but we must hold tight to the anchor that is hope.

God has a plan.

He cares for your needs.

He loves you. It's that simple.

I cannot wait to share with you the story of Mark in book number two of The Lawson Series, *Finding Faith*. Until then, feel free to e-mail me:

rpandfaith@gmail.com

You can also find me on-line at: www.rosepetalsandfaith.weebly.com

Instagram: @RosePetalsAndFaith

Twitter: @KatlynGracee

YouTube: www.youtube.com/c/KatlynGrace

Thanks again for letting me share my first special story with you. God Bless.

Keep Smiling,

Katlyn Grace

about the author

Katlyn Grace resides in a small town in West Virginia and adores spending time with friends and family. She enjoys writing, photography, music, early mornings, and gong on walks. Katlyn also runs a Christian advise blog, *RosePetalsAndFaith*. She writes with the intent to inspire others to follow God and pursue His calling on their lives.